REVOLVER

MARCUS SEDGWICK

SQUARE
FISH

ROARING BROOK PRESS
NEW YORK

SQUARE
FISH

An Imprint of Macmillan

Cataloging-in-Publication Data is on file at the Library of Congress

ISBN 978-0-312-54797-4

Originally published in the United States by Roaring Brook Press
First Square Fish Edition: September 2011
Square Fish logo designed by Filomena Tuosto
macteenbooks.com

10 9 8 7 6 5 4 3 2 1

AR: 5.2 / LEXILE: 890L

For my brother

CONTENTS

1910, Giron

1899, Nome

1910, Giron

1899, Nome

1910, Giron

1967, The Warwick Hotel, New York City

To a professional man, everything is beautiful which shews skill and efficiency in his own particular profession; and thus a murderous weapon is beautiful to a soldier, in proportion to the execution it will commit.

CHAMBERS' EDINBURGH JOURNAL, 1853

The King of Weapons. The Colt Revolver! Adopted by The United States Army, The United States Navy, The National Guard. Used by Mounted Police, Sheriffs, Cowboys and Frontiersmen. The various patterns have been submitted to the most exhaustive tests and pronounced The Safest, The Strongest, The Most Reliable Revolver in the World.

GENERAL ADVERTISEMENT FOR COLTS,
1896

1910

Giron

68 LATITUDE NORTH

1

Wash Day, dusk

Even the dead tell stories.

Sig looked across the cabin to where his father lay, waiting for him to speak, but his father said nothing, because he was dead. Einar Andersson lay on the table, his arms half raised above his head, his legs slightly bent at the knee, frozen in the position in which they'd found him; out on the lake, lying on the ice, with the dogs waiting patiently in harness.

Einar's skin was gray; patches of frost and ice still clung to his beard and eyebrows despite the warmth of the cabin. It was only a matter of degree. Outside the temperature was plunging as night came on, already twenty below, maybe more. Inside the cabin it was a comfortable few degrees above freezing, and yet Einar's body refused to relax from its death throes.

Sig stared and stared, in his own way frozen to the

1

chair, waiting for his father to get up, smile again, and start talking. But he didn't.

They say that dead men tell no tales, but they're wrong. Even the dead tell stories.

2

Wash Day, night

If.
 The smallest word, which raises the biggest questions.
If Sig had been with Einar that morning, what then?
If Einar had been more honest with them, what then?
And what if, what if Einar had taken the Colt with him? Would he still be alive?

Questions began to surface in Sig's mind. The death-spell was breaking. He shivered once, violently, and saw that the stove was nearly out.

He cursed with a short old word, the sort of word his father would have used, but only when his new young wife, Nadya, wasn't around, because she was very strict about these words. And if Anna had heard him, she too would have given him a stern look.

"Father!"

Then she would have laughed. Of course she would

3

have laughed, for she was always laughing, unless she was singing. Unless she was singing, or fighting with Nadya.

Sig waited, though he did not know what he was waiting for. Perhaps a sign of some kind, perhaps even just one single sound, but nothing came, and the only thing he could hear was the sound of his breathing, the breath on the back of his knuckles as he pushed his fist against his lips. Finally he moved from the chair and realized that the shadows had crept across the room and draped it all in darkness. The cabin glowed softly in the light from the single oil lantern hanging from a stout metal hook in the center beam of the roof.

Their cabin. Their entire world, a single room, twenty-four feet by twelve, plus the four feet square of the entrance hall, where the boots and coats waited until it was time for them to work again, and the larder room, which was behind the other inner door in the hall. The larder room, which as well as holding all their food, candles, soap, tools, and spare cloth, was at night home to Sig, who'd taken to sleeping curled up on the sacks of flour. At least it was a little inside space of his own. Outside, there was always all the space in the world; outside, there was nothing but the wide and empty cold of the North. The lake, the forest behind, the mountains in the distance.

Sig lit a taper from the embers of the fire, moving

around the table, trying to decide whether he should look at his father or not. He supposed that when he started thinking of his father not as his father but as a body, that would be the time to stop looking.

He lifted down a smaller lantern from the long shelf over the main window and magicked a flame alight with the taper, which he threw back into the belly of the stove.

In the hall, he pulled on his reindeer-skin boots and gloves, and though he didn't realize it, just the touch of the soft fur of the inverted skin made him feel better.

He shut the inner door to the cabin, put his gloved hand on the outer one, and then hesitated. He took a deep breath, preparing himself for the assault.

He tugged the latch, and before he'd even stepped outside the cold had him, grasping him, squeezing his chest and biting his face. The wind clawed at his mouth and nose, but a hundred miles north of the Arctic Circle, Sig had learned the trick of holding his breath inside until he knew which way the wind was attacking. Still it stole up the backs of his legs and over his face, finding a way in to drain him of his heat.

Dipping his head, he hurried across the newly fallen snow to the log pile and grabbed half a dozen pieces of wood. On his way back, he saw the lake, shining in the light from a bright moon. Somehow he'd expected it to look different, marked by his father's death, but it didn't. He'd seen it look like this a hundred times, and then he understood what was hurting him. It looked commonplace when life had just become anything but. It didn't even occur to him that come the spring when the ice melted, the place where Einar died would disappear completely and become gentle wave crests of the wind-whipped lake once more. But then, when snow covers everything and the mercury shows dozens of degrees below zero, any season but winter is a memory impossible to summon.

As Sig stumbled back into the hall, dropping the logs and pulling off his boots, the question of the lake nagged at him. He gathered up the wood and bumped the inner door of the cabin open, his skin tingling from the sudden increase in warmth.

He made up the fire, wheeling open the air vents to allow the belly of the stove to suck in as much air as it could. Within moments the embers were glowing fiercely, and in a few moments more, they caught some curls of birch bark and the resin underneath almost exploded.

It reminded Sig of what his father had told him once, about what happens in the gun, deep inside the gun, inside the brass casing of the cartridge, when it's fired.

But the ease with which he'd lit the fire also reminded him that his father had failed to light one, which was why he lay frozen behind him on the cabin table.

Why *had* Einar gone across the lake?

He'd taken the four dogs and the small sled to Giron as usual that morning, following the track around the head of the lake, in and out of the trees, snaking around, making the journey from the shack to the town six miles when a crow would have done it in two.

It was Wash Day, and though the miners themselves would work six days, Einar's work for Bergman at the Assay Office occupied only five. On Wash Day, however, Einar always had some business or other to attend to: discussions with Per Bergman, the owner of the mine, or drinks at the bar of the Station Hotel before heading home to his family for what remained of the afternoon.

Sig loved those Wash Day afternoons. His memories of his real mother he could perhaps count on one hand, but his father's new wife, Nadya, would get all the washing and cleaning and other housework done. Then, like Vikings of old, they would take their weekly bath. Nadya and Anna boiled buckets and buckets of water on the stove, and Sig and Einar would make trip after trip to the pump for more. Einar would fetch the tin bath from the hook on the outside back wall of the cabin, while Nadya strung a blanket over a line across the far end of the room.

The girls—Anna, Sig's sister, and Nadya, Einar's wife— would be allowed the hottest and cleanest water, and would go first. They would talk women's gentle talk, if they weren't fighting; they would spit silence at each other if they were. When they'd finished, Einar and Sig would take their turns. Sig loved sitting in the warm water, knees tucked under his chin, watching the snow fall through the end window of the cabin if it were winter, or the shadows moving in the pines if it were summer. What he loved most of all though, was the time spent with his father after the bath, as Nadya and Anna prepared supper.

It was at these times that Einar told Sig important things. The things a son should learn from his father. It was at these times that he told him about the gold days, and the gold lust, or about the revolver, which sat in its original box, like a princess's jewels in a case. And Sig, like a good pupil, would listen, always listen, with maybe a rare question now and again.

"A gun is not a weapon," Einar once said to Sig. "It's an answer. It's an answer to the questions life throws at you when there's no one else to help."

Sig hadn't understood what he meant by that. Not then.

And it was at a time just like this that Einar would say to Sig, "Never cross the lake once you see a hooded crow. They only return when the weather's warming. And never cross the lake by the river mouth; the ice is always thinner there. Even in wintertime."

So why, when Einar had followed his own advice and taken the twisting track around the head of the lake when he went to town that morning, had he come home directly across it?

3

Wash Day, night

"You smell so much nicer now," Anna would tease her little brother, each and every Wash Day. There were enough years between them that they'd never been rivals, only friends, and until Nadya had come along, Anna had been Sig's mother as well as his sister.

These days he felt as if he had two mothers, and God knew there were very few years between the two, with Anna now a woman and Nadya twenty-five years younger than her husband.

But this Wash Day, there had been no bathing, no talk, no laughter, and no Einar.

The three—Sig, Anna, and Nadya—had waited all afternoon, until the bickering between the two women who were not his mother grew so bad that without explaining where he was going Sig decided to head out and look for his father. At least he could meet him halfway home on the track and ride back on the sled.

Maybe Einar would flick the dogs into a run and they'd rush like the north wind through the scrubby trees surrounding the lake.

Even in the depths of winter, Sig spent much time outside, thinking, thinking, thinking. Trying to work out what to do with himself. When they'd arrived in Giron, he'd spent a couple of solitary years in the school the mining company had opened in town, but though he learned a little, he learned little about people. He'd always been the misfit boy, the newcomer, son of the new assay clerk who seemed to think he was too good to live in Giron like the rest of them. Turning fourteen, Sig had left school. Now he had to decide what to do with his life, when in truth there was small choice but to join the mine, like everyone else. From time to time he would help Einar at the Assay Office, but otherwise he chopped wood, mended fences, repaired the cabin, looked after the dogs, and, trying to find himself, got lost in the forests instead. And though he spent much of his time looking, thinking, watching, he could never quite shift the feeling that he was waiting for something.

Maybe it had something to do with the life they'd led. What is it that gets lost, gets lost somewhere in the snow, when you spend almost all your life on the run, with no mother and the cold snapping at your heels every moment of every day of every year?

Whatever it was, Sig didn't even know its name.

11

*

Growing impatient to see his father, he'd shuffled into his boots, then fetched his skis down from the pegs under the eaves at the short side of the cabin, and poled away across the track, glad to be out listening to nothing but silence. His skis had tugged in the snow as he went, and he knew he should have done what his father had been telling him to for days: rub a candle across their flat fat faces.

"Even whalemen rub oil on the bottom of their whaleboats," Einar had said, "so the water doesn't stick. And *you* can't see the point of a little wax on your skis!"

It had been hard going, and Sig was just wondering whether to ignore his father's advice again and risk the much easier and much shorter trip to Giron across the ice, when he looked out across the frozen lake.

He stopped.

There was a black smudge on the ice, a quarter of a mile out, maybe more. His mind slowed for a moment, as it made a connection. He told himself that the smudge could be anything, but he knew this sight: the black on the white. Sometimes there'd be a murder of crows hopping around the smudge, the carcass of a reindeer that had fallen for some reason in the snow. The crows were bold, unafraid of humans, and would only flap lazily away at the last second, as Sig and Einar approached to inspect the dead beast, its ribcage already stripped bare by the birds. Sig remembered the very first time he'd seen such a thing; he'd been perhaps eight years old. His father had beckoned him closer to have a look, but Sig kept his distance, not scared, not upset, but just watching.

It was starting to snow.

He looked up and down the track again, straining his ears, but he could hear nothing. He looked back at the dark blotch on the whiteness. It hadn't moved. With that, he turned his skis and slid down the lake shore.

He tested the first few feet of ice with his pole. It held, but that proved nothing; only his full weight would be a true test. He looked out to the black dot and for a second couldn't see it, then there it was again, slightly off to his left.

Suddenly, despite the cold and the freezing air catching in his nose, he began to prickle with sweat. He had realized something. The smudge lay exactly on a path to the cabin if you were to come straight from Giron, which he could place precisely from the sky-high plume of smoke and steam that rose eternally from the iron works. A path that would go dangerously near the river mouth.

Then Sig knew exactly what had happened.

Heedless of weak ice, ignoring the creaking beneath him, he pushed onto the lake and poled his way with silent desperation toward the smudge. It took very little time for the dot to become a distinct huddle, and then a whole series of shapes.

13

When Fram, the lead dog, saw him, she began to bark a welcome. She stood, and this made the other three dogs get to their feet too, but Sig was staring only at the shape of his father lying on the ice.

The horror of seeing his father frozen to death hammered into him, but there was something worse. As Sig looked frantically but hopelessly around, he pieced together what had happened, and he knew his father had died an utterly pathetic and pitiful death.

His body lay twisted on one side, arms splayed slightly above his head. His legs and the bottom half of his torso shone with the gleam of ice, the rest of him did not. For some reason he had taken one of his gloves off, a ridiculous thing to do in this cold. His Assay Office satchel lay on the ice, and then Sig saw the little matchbox, and the jumble of matches near his father's hands, which looked like a microscopic version of the logjams the timbermen make on the river in summertime.

None of it made sense until Sig saw what a stranger to the North might have missed. A slight disturbance, a couple of jagged edges with less frost aging than the rest, sticking up out of a patch of ice. Sig knew what it was.

It was the weak spot on the ice, the hole his father had fallen through, a hole from which he had somehow managed to scramble out and which had already frozen over again in the merciless cold.

The ice on Einar's body showed he had fallen in up to his waist, perhaps his chest. If he had gone right in, the lake would never have let him go again, and even so it must have taken a heroic effort to drag himself free.

Sig saw the whole scene now as if he'd been there.

He saw his father pulling on the ganglines of the dogs' harnesses, the dogs themselves fighting to stay on their feet, claws scraping frantically. Somehow he gets enough of his body out of the hole and hauls his legs up after him. He knows he has to work fast. His clothes are already freezing onto him, and though home is only a mile distant, he'll be dead before he gets halfway. Unless he can make a fire.

He has no wood, but then he sees clearly. The sled is made of wood; there are papers from the mine office in his leather satchel. And he's got matches. But with gloved hands he can't even get the box out of his pocket.

He risks pulling off one glove with his teeth and fishes the box from inside his fur-lined parka, but it's bad now, his body is shuddering with great convulsions, as the ice forming on his legs and feet greedily sucks away his body heat. He drops the matchbox in the snow and, kneeling down, it takes many attempts just to get his fingers, already numb, to close around it.

At last, at last, he holds it fast, then realizes he should have got the papers and broken up the sled first. He wants to cry, but he can't. He can't even think straight.

15

He pulls at his satchel with his gloved left hand, but even that is hard because he can no longer control the muscles in his arms.

Knowing his chances are slipping away, he pushes the matchbox open, but then he shivers and pushes too far. Box and tray separate and all the tiny wooden lifelines spill into the inch of snow on the frozen lake.

Sig sees it all, just as if he'd been there. He knows he'll never forget it to the end of his own days. He wonders what it's like to die. To die alone.

Now, Einar knows he's dead. He can't pick the matches up with his bulky, shaking gloved hand, and he can't pick them up with his free hand because it has frozen into an unworking claw. Frantically he tries to push the heads of the matches against the striking paper on the side of the box. He tries to use his lips to pick them up, but it's no good; he's lost all feeling in his face.

Finally, with a hideous irony, his fumblings against the box randomly strike head against paper, and a small chemical miracle invented by some Swedes, involving among other things glass, phosphorous, sulphur, and potassium, occurs out there on the frozen lake in the middle of a Northern nowhere. A single splutter of flame catches as the match head ignites, lying on the ice. It burns halfway down the wooden stalk of the match, and all Einar can do is watch it burn for a second, and then die.

An hour later, and he's dead too.

4

Sun Day, early morning

"Have faith. Be brave, Sig," Anna had said, and they'd gone, leaving him with Einar. He rubbed the back of his neck with one hand, then stopped himself, remembering it was a gesture of his father's.

Sig had heard stories that when you freeze to death, the last thing you feel is a wonderful warmth spread through your whole body, filling you with joy. He hoped it was like that for his father, but a bit of him, in the corner of his mind, wondered how anyone actually knows. Again he was reminded of his father, who would always say, "Know what you can. Know *everything* you can know."

All Sig knew as he knelt by his father was that suddenly there had been the sound of skis shushing up behind him, and Anna and Nadya were there.

He remembered little of the hurried plans. Anna and Nadya had come fully dressed for the snow; they'd seen Sig on the ice and had rushed out to intercept him. The

17

snow sifted down at them insistently, and hesitantly they managed to lift Einar onto the sled, trying to suppress their panic, pushing aside the shock of seeing Einar dead. The ice had complained and whined, yet none of them spoke of the sudden frozen end that could take them at any moment. With Einar on the sled, they made it to the cabin, running onto the land before the creaking and cracking could shatter their nerve entirely.

There had been a short, silent standoff as they wondered who should go and who should stay, and in the end, Sig, seeing the discomfort on his sister's face, had said, "You two go. I'll wait."

Nadya squeezed his hand.

"Bravely done," she whispered.

Then the two women had gone to town for help.

"Be brave," Anna had said. She was trying not to cry. Nadya had said nothing. There was an empty look in her eyes as if the cold landscape had taken possession of them. They'd set off with the dogs once again, Anna driving the team, standing on the runners, Nadya sitting where Einar had lain. Sig watched them vanish, and between the smoky trees and the gray snow in the dusk, they vanished very quickly indeed. He headed back to the cabin.

He'd closed the fire down a little before going to bed, now that it was full of food and eating slowly but happily. He looked at the narrow bed where Einar and Nadya slept, and at the bench where Anna put her mattress every night. He had a choice of beds now.

Then he looked at his father on the table, and he opted for his sacks of flour in the freezing larder, leaving the warmth of the cabin to the corpse.

In the pale morning, rubbing his arms to get the blood moving, Sig stumbled into the light.

His father had moved. He looked as though he were sleeping, turned on one side with his arms and legs now gently folded beside him.

Sig rushed over to the table, a stupid hope rising to his lips, and then he saw his father's face, and he knew he hadn't come back to life. His body had simply thawed and relaxed, the rigor mortis passing too, but there was no life in his eyes, nor breath in his mouth, already starting to pinch into a death mask.

Sig collapsed back onto the chair behind him and stifled the tears that began to burn in his eyes, because he understood it would not help to cry.

Then there was a knock at the door.

It wasn't God or the Declaration of Independence that made all men equal. It was Samuel Colt.

ANON

1899

Nome

66 LATITUDE NORTH

5

Frontier

Agreed brought them, and now it seemed as if that greed would kill them. Ice-bitten and hunger-eyed, Einar Andersson stood on the beach, very near the creek that had started the whole damn thing, and wept. It had been his greed, his weakness, and it was his guilt that he fought to ignore now.

Tears froze to his eyelashes and his cheeks, and he rubbed them away with a sealskin-gloved hand before they could frostbite him.

Away, almost on the horizon now, was the boat.

He had pleaded with the captain, pleaded, begged, offered bribes he did not have, and all for nothing.

The captain was not a bad man. Einar knew that. But though the captain was not a bad man, he was a stubborn one, a quality perhaps a ship's captain needs when sailing northern seas.

He'd given Einar the chance to speak, at least. Many would not even have bothered with that courtesy in this faith-deserted place, but the captain had stood on the beach beside the very last rowboat to put out to the ship.

"What would you have me do, Einar?"

The captain put a thick-gloved hand on Einar's shoulder. Einar pushed it away.

"She's dying. Don't you understand? She's dying."

The captain looked at the ice-rimed stones on the beach, shaking his head. He turned and barked orders to his men, then spoke quietly to Einar.

"Then I am sorry, sir, but your wife is already dead. God be with you."

He turned to go and Einar grabbed wildly at his arm.

"Wait!" he cried. "Please! A day or two and, God willing, she'll be well enough to move."

The captain tugged his arm free, scowling at Einar.

"What would you have me do?" he repeated, angrily this time. He jabbed his hand toward the sea horizon.

"The life of your wife against two hundred and fifty souls on that boat? Is it a gamble you want me to take?"

Einar opened his mouth but could not think what to say. He closed it again and watched as the captain stepped over the stern of the long rowboat even as his men shoved it into the near-freezing water, its motions already slowing in the plummeting cold. Very soon, the captain knew, and Einar knew, the water would slow to the point where it froze, froze solid in strange waves and ridges near the shore, smoothing to form an ice sheet that within a few weeks would reach clear across the Norton Sound and far out into the Bering Sea, to the Pribilov Islands, over five hundred miles away.

Now Einar watched the boat go.

The last boat. There would not be another for seven months. Not until the ice melted in the late spring.

The boat dwindled, barely seeming to move yet getting smaller with every second. In the stillness of the late morning, the sounds carried across the sea with ease. He heard the tolling of the ship's bell, and he remembered it was Sunday. In his mind he saw the pastor calling the faithful to a secluded corner of the deck for prayer, asking the Lord for safe passage to their destination, two thousand miles and more to the south.

Einar watched the boat go, as some stubbornness of his own told him that whatever might happen in the next seven months, he'd be standing on this beach when the first boats returned. He would nurse Maria to one ending or another, but whatever else, he would stand on that beach next May, as if he'd never moved from the spot.

Suddenly he realized the boat was no longer there to be seen.

So. He turned his back on the sea and looked at the Cape Nome Mining Camp. A few dozen tents. A handful of clapboard shacks formed what was optimistically being called Front Street, as if this place was a town.

Their home for the next seven months. At least one of the shacks was theirs. They might just make it. As for Maria, only God knew, but then with a surge of fear tightening his throat, he thought of the children.

Little Anna, only ten, and—heaven!—his boy, Sigfried, half that.

He put his head down and walked back up the beach, hearing a last toll of the ship's bell as he went.

Greed had brought him; only Faith would save them.

Mobs and murderers appear to rule the hour. The revolver rules, the revolver is triumphant.

WALT WHITMAN, 1857

1910

Giron

68 LATITUDE NORTH

6

Sun Day, morning

"Son?"

It was a strange first word to utter, and it wasn't meant as any name or manner of introduction. It was an interrogation, a question, and it meant, *Are you the son of Einar Andersson?*

Sig looked up into the face of the man who'd knocked on the door. This in itself was odd, since no one ever knocked on their door. Only once in their three years in Giron had anyone come calling—Per Bergman, the chattering owner of the mine, and he'd come by special arrangement to share lunch one Sun Day.

No one else came by, and otherwise Einar, Nadya, Anna, and Sig would announce their arrival by the stamp of their boots on the porch.

"The Andersson boy?"

Mute as a tomb, Sig stared at the man. He made to push past Sig, who for some reason found he'd wedged

33

his foot against the inside of the door. The door shoved against it, but it resisted.

The man was a giant. Behind him in the yard between the cabin, the outhouse, and the dog huts, stood a giant horse, breathing great clouds of steam into the morning air. The frost crackled in the trees, and a crow cawed a harsh call across the frozen lake. The first crow of the year.

The man's face was like nothing Sig had ever seen, even in their years of travels around the rim of the world. He'd seen the Esquimaux and the Athabaskans; he'd seen Samoyedes and Sami, but he'd never seen anyone look like the man at the door. His features were coarse, his eyes far apart, his nose broad, his mouth hidden by a rough beard of ginger and white. His head, when he removed his fur hat, was shaven to his scalp. His skull was a disturbing shape, flat at the back, his ears too small. It was not a face stroked into creation by God's loving hand, but battered into shape by the Devil's hammer.

He pulled off a glove and put a fist of meat against the edge of the door, and Sig knew he could pull it off its hinges if he wanted to. With a twitch of his lip, Sig noticed that the man was missing the thumb of his left hand.

"Who are you?" Sig said, dragging his eyes away from the deformity, breaking the silence. "Have you come to help?"

He looked past the man, hoping to see Anna and Nadya there, putting the dogs away, having brought help. But his sister and stepmother were nowhere in sight.

The man leaned forward, looking past Sig into the cabin. His heavy black-skin greatcoat swung aside like a theater curtain, ushering on stage a new character.

There, in the inky shadow at the man's hip, sat the butt and grip of a revolver.

"Einar?" said the man. It was all he needed to say.

"No. No," said Sig hurriedly, panic rising inside him. "No, he's not here. He'll be back."

The man kept staring over his shoulder.

"When?"

Sig tried to place his accent but with so little to go on, it was hard to tell. He might have come from any country of the North; he might be American, maybe Dutch-American, maybe German. But the man was waiting for an answer, and the longer he left it, the more obvious Sig's lies would seem.

"Don't know. Later. Maybe."

"I'll wait."

For a moment it seemed as if the man would barge past him into the cabin, but instead, he turned, slowly mounting his horse, flicking the beast to a walk. He was looking straight ahead, back at the path to town, but then his gaze shot to Sig, just as he was about to close the door.

"Alone?"

And for some reason, Sig could only tell the truth this time.

"Yes," he said, though the word died in his throat.

The man nodded.

7

Sun Day, noon

Y ou might never know what it was that killed you. You might not see it coming; it might strike like the proverbial lightning bolt from the blue.

Or you might have some inkling of your doom. You might suspect the cause; that it is your greed or your lust for revenge or your blind faith that is to be your undoing.

Or you might see it clearly, running over the horizon toward you. Death on a pale horse.

Sig spent all morning pounding the blade of the shovel through the snow to the icy ground beneath. The snow was cleared in moments, but after an hour of frantic attempts to dig a hole, the tongue of the shovel gave up and snapped, the old metal fatigued in the cold, the ground as hard as bitterness.

He'd been standing in the cabin, and more and more,

had been unable to take his eyes off the corpse. Suddenly the vision from the day before returned, and he saw his father as the reindeer carcass, his ribs picked clean, and a deep cavity already hollowed out behind them by ravenous birds. He couldn't bear it and had rushed out to find the shovel, intent on burying the thing that had been his father.

Now, exhausted, he collapsed sobbing in the snow, his hands scraping at the grave he'd tried to dig for Einar, a dozen inches across, and a few less deep. Angrily he threw the handle of the shovel away behind the dog huts. He picked up the blade to follow it, then felt the anger drop from him, and with it let the blade fall in the snow by his feet.

But what was he going to do with the body?

Surely Anna and Nadya should have returned by now? At least Anna should. And Nadya, too. Of course she would come back.

But into his mind came the sight and sounds of their jealous fights, tongues spiteful and eyes cruel, when he couldn't believe he was seeing his singing sister before him. Sig, innocent and young, could never understand why they argued over Maria, so long gone. And the things Anna said about Nadya were harsh, and not true, not true, but where then, was she now?

He shook his head and stood, pushing the doubts away.

If Nadya had wanted to leave, she could have done so at any moment in the last couple of years, and she certainly hadn't stayed for Einar's wealth; they owned nothing, even the cabin they lived in, the tools they used, the food they ate, it all came from the mine, from the Company. The Company owned everything.

Any minute now, Sig told himself, both Anna and Nadya would appear around the track, bringing some company men to help them.

Sig staggered back into the cabin, shattered, dragging his boots off as he closed the inner door behind him. He tried not to look across at his father on the table, but he couldn't help it. He had to do something. He pulled a blanket from Einar and Nadya's bed and threw it across the body, trying but failing to avoid his father's eyes, which were still open, giving Sig the terrible feeling that Einar was watching him from beyond death.

With the body covered, he tried to roll it over to adopt a more natural position. Then he gently rearranged the blanket into a more fitting shroud.

With a moan in his heart he saw that the logs were almost eaten up, and turned to the door, when through the window he saw someone.

There, framed like an oil painting, sat the man on his horse. It was a pale horse.

The man stared right through the glass at Sig, then he

swung his leg over the beast's back and dismounted. Sig again caught a flash of the nickel backstrap.

The man walked steadily toward the cabin door.

These men are mad with lust for Gold. Conditions will be desperate unless a restraining influence can be exerted. You can hardly imagine to what depths a mining camp, shut away from civilization for eight months by a thousand miles of impassable ice, may descend.

GOVERNOR JOHN G. BRADY
GOVERNOR OF ALASKA.
1897–1906

1899

Nome

66 LATITUDE NORTH

8

Faith

"May God protect us now."

Einar always remembered the first words Maria whispered when she learned that the boat had sailed without them.

He'd come for the gold, and he hadn't meant to stay. These things never lasted long, Einar knew. Just like the Klondike, by the time the rest of the world got to know about the gold, it would be too late; all the best strikes found, the land claimed, the easy pickings gone. All that would be left would be the struggle to survive in a world of danger, both natural and man-made, with the occasional speck of gold dust coming his way. Just enough to keep that stupid dream of easy money alive, the dream of fantastic wealth, of ease and luxury and fine things for the rest of his days, but in reality not enough to live on for even a week.

"Yes, my love," Einar said, sitting down on the floor by the makeshift cabin bed, stroking Maria's forehead. Sig lay curled up by her feet. There was nowhere else for him to sleep. Anna stood, holding a ragged old doll, hopping from one foot to the other, trying to see through the frost-rimmed window, stealing a glance at her mother from time to time, trying not to think thoughts she didn't like.

"Yes, my love," Einar said softly. "God will protect us now."

Maria's fever was high again, and sweat poured from her face though she shuddered as if icy winds gripped her. Suddenly she winced, screwing up her face, her eyes shut fast.

"Anna," Einar called. "See to the fire."

The girl stared at her mother, not hearing her father.

"Anna!" he called, louder now. "Anna, make up the fire. We must keep your mother warm."

Still she ignored him. She hopped onto her other foot and began to stroke her doll's tattered dress and wooden head, with its few strands of real horsehair.

"Anna!" Einar shouted this time.

She jumped and stood straight like a soldier but still didn't move. Sig woke and almost immediately began to cry.

Einar cursed and shook his head.

"Anna," he said, more softly. "Anna, see to your brother while I see to the fire."

Anna nodded, dropping her doll onto the bare wooden floor and picking up her little brother bodily. She was tall for her age, he was small for his, and she held him like a baby against her chest, singing to him, till she could hold him no more.

She put him down and with surprise saw her mother looking at her, a weak smile on her lips.

"Have faith," she whispered, so quietly that Anna didn't really hear.

9

The Frozen Sea

Never was there a winter like the winter in Nome as, somewhere over the course of seven months, 1899 became 1900.

As the sea froze, a great cavernous silence descended on the town, an eerie nothingness, in which the few sounds there were traveled unnaturally far. It froze so hard that the enormous pressure of ice from far out to sea threw huge slabs of shore ice up onto the beach, twenty feet, thirty feet, even fifty feet. The Esquimaux called it *ivu*, "the ice that leaps," but Einar took it as another strange omen of the desolate world to which he had foolishly brought his family.

Was it good providence or bad that his cousin was a friend of one of the Three Lucky Swedes, the infamous trio who'd been sent to breed reindeer as an alternative food source for the Esquimaux but had instead found a hunk of gold the size of a man's head?

Good or bad?

Einar and his family had been among the very first to arrive that summer, eager for a quick strike and retreat before the hordes descended. But Einar had found nothing, then winter had closed in just as Maria got ill, stranding them. Einar could do nothing to support them. While some men still tried to prospect for gold through the early winter, even if only by stalking along the beach hoping to repeat the Swedes' success, Einar had to stay with his family.

His were the only children in Nome, his was the only white woman. There had already been a death from a fight over a local woman, and aside from that Einar knew he couldn't leave Anna to look after both her brother and her mother for more than an hour or so.

Later that week, another man was found behind the dog sheds with his throat slit, all for a pinch of tobacco, someone said.

So they clung to the inside of the shack, and as the price of coal went to a hundred dollars a ton, and eggs to ten dollars a dozen, Einar spent their last twenty dollars buying a slim but broad box from an old-timer, who went and drank the whole twenty dollars worth in whisky at the half-built building that was to become Dexter's saloon.

Anna stared at her father as he stomped back into the cabin with the box.

"What's that, Pappa?" she whispered, her eyes wide.

Maria woke and propped herself up. Her movement disturbed Sig, who woke too, to witness one of the few scenes from his early childhood that he would remember forever, and clearly.

He remembered the look on his mother's face as she saw what Einar had bought. Only many years later would he finally be able to put a word to that look. Despair.

"What is it?" Anna repeated. "Is it food? Is it for when the food runs out?"

"No," Einar muttered. "It's something else. For when the faith runs out."

10

Cabin Fever

Know what you will of the world. Know what you can, know what men are and the things they do. Understand what God is to you, understand what you are to your loved ones. Love, sing, cry, and fight, but all the time, seek to know everything you can about the earth upon which you stand, till your time is done.

Both Einar and Maria had tried to teach Sig this same message. It was simply that they went about it in very different ways, and sometimes, like all parents, they both failed to teach their children anything at all.

At the darkest point that winter, when the sun barely rose in the sky, and then only for a couple of hours each day, the stores of food under the bed ran out.

Maria slept fitfully, her Bible by her side, its gold edging gleaming from between the battered black leather covers.

At about five o'clock one afternoon, in pitch darkness, Einar Andersson strode across Front Street, heading for the saloon. His hand opened and closed on something tucked into the waistband of his trousers, hidden under his sealskin coat.

Anna watched him go through a spy hole she'd scraped in the ice on the inside of the window. Sig stood by the table, just tall enough to peer into the box that Pappa had left there, its lid open. The inside of the box was organized into special shapes and compartments, all lined with short, dusty velvet. Whatever had been in there was gone, leaving behind a long triangular hole, a few unfamiliar metal objects, a little brush, a tiny tin of oil.

Sig reached toward the box, fascinated.

"Sig," Anna called from the window. "Don't touch that. Come here and watch with me."

Sig's hand hovered in midair above the box, but then he did as he was told and silently trotted over to join his sister at the window.

"Where's Pappa?" he said, after a while.

"Gone out."

"What's he doing?"

"I don't know."

"Has he gone to get us something to eat?"

Anna paused. The two of them stared out of the window.

"Yes," she said. "I think so."

52

11

Peacemaker

How things unwind.

Mean and makeshift, the black heart of the brawling, gambling, thieving, starving slop bucket of Nome was its half-built saloon. With no way out of the camp, even those with money or gold had soon realized that they couldn't buy food or drink if there's none to be had, and the saloon was the last supply of both.

Einar went up to the bar, a few eyes on him, but many too absorbed in their own problems to worry about the idiot who'd brought two kids and a woman who wasn't a whore to this hellhole.

He stood at the bar.

The barkeep, a thin, surly man called Jack, wandered over, wiping the bar top with his cloth as he came, as if this were some fancy joint in San Francisco with a mahogany counter, not three planks nailed to the top of a couple of filthy barrels.

"Einar?"

"Drink."

"Whisky or gin?"

"Gin."

Jack plonked a bottle without a label and a dirty glass down on the bar, and Einar helped himself to a long drink. His hand was shaking, and he spilled some on the rough-grained wood.

"Hey," said Jack. "It's not like we have any to spare."

He grumbled, wiping the mess while Einar drank the whole thing in one go. He set the glass back down and immediately began to refill it.

"Dollar," said Jack, taking the bottle from Einar's hand before he could spill any more.

"And another for that," the barkeep added. "Two dollars."

Einar lifted the glass to his lips and drank it down in one swallow again.

"I don't have any money, Jack," he said quietly.

"What you say?"

"I said, I don't have any more money. Or any gold. Or any food. I have a wife and a daughter and my boy, but I don't have any money."

"You have to pay for that drink," Jack said, his face clouding. "You have to pay for both of them, or what's to happen next, if people don't pay."

Einar shrugged.

"Hey!" Jack cried, grabbing Einar's sleeve.

"What's the matter?" said a voice at Einar's shoulder, and he turned to see a man whose face was familiar but whose name he didn't know.

"Won't pay for his drink," Jack snarled.

"That so?" said the man, his voice level and his face impassive.

Jack still held Einar's sleeve, but imperceptibly Einar began to edge his other hand behind him, under his coat, his fingertips feeling for the heel of the grip.

Suddenly Einar felt himself whipped around, as the stranger spun him as easily as a top. There was a loud slap on the counter, followed a moment later by a second, lighter one, with the tinkle of metal.

"You looking for this?" the man said, glaring at Einar.

On the bar top sat Einar's revolver, still rocking from the force with which the man had set it there. Next to it lay three dollars. The man shoved the coins at Jack.

"That's for his, and for the one you're about to pour for me."

Jack poured a shot and went off grumbling, taking the bottle with him.

Einar made to take back his gun, but the man caught his wrist.

"You fool. What are you doing, walking in here with that thing?"

Einar shrugged again.

"Is that your answer to everything?"

"I don't know what to say," Einar said. "I . . . I don't know what to do."

"So you came in here trying to get your head blown off?"

"No . . ."

"No? Or were you going to stage a heist all by yourself? Once someone starts shooting in this place, every gun in the room is going to get warm. Then we might as well all lie down in the snow and die."

He picked up the gun.

"Colt Single Action Army, 1873 model. The Peacemaker." He smiled. "This particular piece must be near to twenty years old."

"You know your guns," Einar conceded.

"I know more than guns, Einar. And I know enough about *them* not to bring one into a place like this unless you mean to kill or be killed."

"So, what would you have me do?" Einar said, anger stinging his voice.

The man smiled.

"Have a little faith," he said.

"So my wife's always telling me."

"Then she's right."

"She's dying."

"I know. Maybe she's dying, maybe she's not, but either way, you got those two lovely kids."

56

Einar's eyes darkened, but the man raised a palm.

"Easy, Einar," he said. "No one's going to hurt your kids. And they're not going to starve."

"Why not?"

"Because I'm going to give you a job."

12

Silence

"I start in the spring," Einar explained to Maria when he got back. "Mr. Salisbury works for the government. Governor Brady sent him in when they heard about the rush. You know that man who got knifed? I told you about it. He was going to be the Assay Clerk. Now they've got no one."

"What's an Assay Clerk?" Anna asked.

"He's a man who tests the gold. He sees how pure it is. The purer it is, the more it's worth. Every town needs an Assay Office, and this place is going to have one. And I'm going to be the man who does the testing and the weighing and the paying."

Maria smiled.

"But how will that help us now?"

"He's given me some money; they're going to bring some food over later on. We're going to be all right. We . . ."

He stopped, catching himself. He looked down into

the dim eyes and gray face of his wife and didn't know what to say.

"That's all right," she whispered. "That's all right. It will be all right. You'll see. Have faith in God."

Einar smiled. With great effort, Maria propped herself up.

"But why did he choose you?" she asked.

"Well, that's the thing. He said he chose me because he says the only man you can trust in a town like this is one who's got too much to lose."

Maria looked blankly at him.

"You three," Einar said, laughing. "You and the children. He said he could trust a family man. See? You two have been some use after all!"

He pulled Anna toward him and gave her a hug. She felt the bristles of his beard against her cheek and giggled.

"Here, son," Einar said to little Sig. "Here's a job for you. Take this and put it back in that box. Carefully. Understand?"

He pulled the Colt from his waistband and handed it to Sig, who beamed at his father. An almost comical solemnity came into the little boy's face, and he walked steadily off to do his job, holding the gun before him as if it were as fragile as a dream.

"Einar!" Maria cried. "No! You mustn't let him touch it. You mustn't. Guns are evil. Evil, Einar."

Einar laughed.

"The boy must learn respect for it while he's young."

"No," Maria said, her anger wearing her out so quickly. "No, he mustn't . . . My children must not know evil things. They must learn to trust in the love and the care of God."

Sig ran back to Einar.

"I did it!" he cried happily. "I did it."

"Good boy," Einar said, ruffling Sig's blond mop of hair.

Silently, Maria turned her face to the wall.

"Good boy," Einar repeated.

"Pappa," Sig said, a puzzled look on his face.

"Yes?"

"The thing in the box."

"Yes?"

"What is it?"

13

The Call of the Wild

"Love," Maria said to her children on the day she got out of bed for the first time. She held up her black Bible, brandishing it as if it could speak for her. "God teaches us many virtues. Above all, he teaches us faith, hope, and love. It was our faith that kept God with us through the darkest times. It was our hope that brought Mr. Salisbury to your father and gave him the job, but both of these would not have been possible without God's love. The Bible teaches us that faith, hope, and love abide. These three, and the greatest of these is love."

It had seemed as if the spring would never come, but for weeks now there had been the first signs of its approach. The frozen sea began to send loud and mysterious noises across the ice, breaking the unnatural stillness. Creaks and groans of ice starting to break shattered the air every now and again. There were more birds in the sky, and the

Esquimaux began to gather in their own camp farther along the shore, cautiously content to trade with the miners, offering fresh meat and seal oil in return for drink and gold and trinkets.

The little community had survived, and though more than a few had died from alcohol or a bullet or starvation, Maria had got better.

Far out to sea, the ships were gathering.

For now, news of the Swedes' gold strike had spread not only to the Yukon and the Klondike, but right across America. Ships had sailed from Seattle, even from distant San Francisco, having waited all winter until it was time to set out.

Even though they had waited, they arrived too soon, and four miles of ice kept the newcomers from the beaches they believed to be strewn with gold. Fifty ships, maybe sixty, lay moored, waiting for the ice to break, to melt.

Every day, Einar would spend an hour or so on the shore, watching as the boats edged a little closer.

One day, there was the sound of shouting and dogs barking from way out on the ice. After two months on board ship, someone had clearly lost his patience at having to wait a few more days at the ice barrier.

Shouts rose and fell, the barking of a dog team hauling on the ice reached Einar, and then suddenly the barking was gone, and the speck that had been the dog team and the rash prospector was gone too.

62

The shouting from the watching ships grew louder for a while, but all too soon it faded away.

Einar shook his head. How foolish to attempt to cross ice that is starting to break. There would be no more impatience of that sort, Einar thought, but what a way to go. What a way to go.

Finally, the last of the ice was no more than a thin, glasslike crust, with a heaving green sea eager to get out from beneath it, and the ships weighed anchor and headed as close to land as they could get.

Just as he'd promised himself the day the last ship left, Einar went down to the shore, joined by Mr. Salisbury and a few of the others who'd survived the winter, to wait for the rowboats to pull their way in the final half mile to the beach.

They came fast, hordes of them like swarming flies, and as keel after keel crunched onto the stones, none of them noticed the desperation in the survivors' eyes, or their faces, haunted and drawn.

They ran like rabid dogs up and down the beach, pushing each other out of the way, scrabbling through the stones, some heaving picks at the ground, hunting for the gold they'd been promised was there for the taking, just lying on the beach.

As the panic subsided, as the rabble began to realize the terrible mistake they'd made, one, an old miner by the look of him, came up to Einar and Mr. Salisbury.

He shook his head and dropped to his hands and knees in front of them.

"It's all a lie!" he cried.

Mr. Salisbury put out a hand, but he was not fast enough to stop the old-timer from pulling his pistol.

He shot himself in the head.

It was on that day that Einar saw him for the first time.

A giant of a man, a bear in human form, haggard and hairy, with fists like hams. He walked through the rowdy rabble, stepping over the body of the suicide as if it were nothing more than a piece of driftwood.

He stared at Mr. Salisbury, then yanked off a glove to jab a stumpy finger at him.

"Where do I get a drink?" he growled.

Einar noticed the newcomer had no thumb on his left hand.

I have no hesitation in declaring the Colt's revolver superior in most respects, and much better adapted to the wants of the Army than the Smith and Wesson.

JOHN R. EDIE
CAPTAIN OF ORDNANCE
ORDNANCE NOTES, NO V.
WASHINGTON, JUNE 27TH, 1873

1910

Giron

68 LATITUDE NORTH

14

Sun Day, noon

"You can wait outside," Sig said, but there was as much chance of that as the King of England's paying a call.

The man didn't debate with Sig but strode through the outer door so forcefully that Sig had to press himself against it to avoid being knocked down.

Sig wasn't quite sure why he had lied about his father, but it was too late now. He followed the man into the cabin, closing the inner door. The room grew darker, and though the mound on the table seemed like a mountain to Sig, incredibly the stranger appeared not to have noticed it.

He spun around to face Sig.

"Gunther Wolff."

Silence. Sig stared at the man, though he would rather have looked anywhere else in the room. He couldn't take his eyes off the visitor.

"Mean anything?" Wolff said, almost whispering, using no more words than were absolutely necessary.

Sig shook his head, lifting his hand to rub the back of his neck. He stopped himself.

Wolff grunted.

"Too young," he said, reasoning to himself. "And too long ago, maybe."

"What do you want?" Sig asked, but Wolff ignored this question.

"You don't remember me. I remember you."

The words hung in the air, drifted around the room. They seemed to paint themselves on the walls in letters two feet high. They seemed to be painted in blood.

"Ten years."

Sig's mind struggled. Ten years . . . that would mean . . .

"Nome. I knew you in Nome. Little then."

Sig nodded. From nowhere, he was suddenly overwhelmed by the loss of his father. He fought to turn his thoughts back to the stranger.

"Did you know my father?"

Wolff filled the room like a threat, ominous, sinister and unknowable. He was covered almost entirely by his long leather greatcoat, once stark black but now a softer, mottled thing of shadows. His face still unsettled Sig, and now he realized it was the man's eyes that had this effect on him. The lower half of Wolff's face was obscured by his beard, and as he pulled the wide-brimmed hat from his head, Sig saw again that he either was bald or had shaved his head to the scalp.

"Did?" he said.

Sig spotted his mistake but saw an explanation.

"In Nome. Did you know him in Nome?"

"Oh, yes," said Wolff, and smiled.

Sig wanted to be sick.

"Oh, yes. I knew your father. And your mother. And the little girl. What was her name . . . ?"

"Anna," Sig said, and as before when he'd admitted he was on his own in the cabin, he regretted giving even Anna's name to Wolff.

"Anna," Wolff repeated. He seemed to be mulling something over, calculating perhaps, and then he blew Sig's game wide open.

"Is that your Pappa under the blanket, boy?"

15

Sun Day, after noon

"Please put that back," Sig said.

Once again Wolff ignored him. He held the hem of the blanket with his one thumb and forefinger, lifting it high enough to expose Einar's sagging face. Almost a day had passed since his death, and already it showed, his skin withering, sallow and gray, sinking, shrinking, his mouth pinching ever tauter.

"Please," Sig said again. "Please put that back."

There was something truly awful in the way Wolff ignored Sig. With a twinge of fear, Sig realized that it spoke of a complete absence of any need to follow rules. A man who will defile the sanctity of the dead will surely think nothing of breaking any of the laws of the land or the laws of God.

"Einar," Wolff whispered, so softly that Sig wasn't sure of what he heard. "Einar. You have cheated me, but you won't win."

Sig stood halfway across the room, glancing out of the window toward the lake and, ultimately, the town. The view looked as it always did in winter; the domination of the white of the snow, the black-brown of trees the only other color. He imagined running away through the trees, hearing the snow crunch underneath his boots, feeling the peeling bark of a birch tree under his gloved hand as he rounded a corner, seeing the strange orange-stained icicles hanging from outcrops of rock, divulging the secret of the ore that lay in the earth, the reason they were all here.

He couldn't see the stranger's horse anymore. Maybe he'd put it in the barn; maybe it was tied up somewhere. Sig hoped it was in the barn; the cold of Giron was no place for a horse, and he wondered how many animals had died beneath Wolff on his journey.

Sig jumped as Wolff suddenly dropped the blanket and turned back toward him.

"When?"

Sig knew what he meant.

"Yesterday. About this time yesterday. He was coming across the ice; it must have broken. I found him, then . . ."

He stopped himself. He didn't want to say their names to this man. But why not? Why should it matter if he mentioned Anna and Nadya?

Wolff stared at Sig, waiting for him to go on. A huge compulsion rose in Sig to blurt out the rest of it, but he

73

fought it. He couldn't, however, hold Wolff's gaze and found himself staring at the floorboards. A memory came into his mind of Anna and Nadya kneeling side by side on the floor, rocking back and forth, scrubbing the black floorboards last spring. Anna would have been singing, Nadya silent. It was one of the few times he could remember them getting along so easily.

And now, where were they? What was taking them so long?

"I have . . ." Wolff stopped, correcting himself. "I had . . . some business to attend to. With your father."

Sig opened and shut his mouth, then opened it again.

"Oh, I see," he said carefully. "Well, I'm sorry that your trip was wasted."

His nerve was weak, but he continued while he had the chance. He felt like he was hearing someone else say the words, as if he had left his own body.

"So, I expect you'll want to be getting along now, before it gets dark."

Wolff pulled a chair from the table upon which Sig's dead father lay.

"Coffee," he said. "Want coffee."

He folded his arms and thrust his booted feet out in front of him on the boards. Reaching around behind him, he set his hat down to rest on the barrel of Einar's blanketed chest.

Sig felt himself go cold inside.

He walked toward Wolff deliberately, trying not to tremble, and lifted the hat from his father's body. He carried it over to the hooks on the beam nearest the door and hung it there as calmly as he could.

"Coffee," Sig said. "Yes, I can make you some coffee before you go."

All the while, Wolff watched him. Sig snatched only a glimpse of his face, and still it was unreadable, or was that, my God, a trace of amusement on Wolff's lips? Sig would almost have preferred to see irritation, even anger, than sense that he was being toyed with.

Sig opened the belly of the stove and threw another small split log inside. The door closed with a satisfying *whump,* and he heard the log crack as the heat from the stove tore into it.

He filled the kettle from the water can and put it on the top of the stove, then made for the inner cabin door.

"Stop," said Wolff, and Sig stopped, his hand already on the door latch. "Where?"

"Coffee's in the storeroom," Sig said. "Just there."

He nodded toward the cabin wall.

"Go on," Wolff grunted, and Sig felt the rock in the pit of his stomach grow heavier. Was he a prisoner now, in his own home?

He made his way through the inner door of the cabin, and while every instinct urged him to rush outside, he instead turned to his right and pushed into the darkness

75

of the storeroom. It had no window, just a small row of adjustable slats high up on the short north wall so that it would be cool even in the brief but fierce summer. With the door ajar, there was enough light to see, and besides, he knew where everything was in that room, even in the dark.

He knew where the sacks of flour and meal on which he slept were. He knew where the butter was kept, and the honey and the coffee. He put up his hand and pulled down the coffee tin, and knew that behind it lay a long, slim, flat wooden box, one that had traveled halfway around the rim of the world with them over the last ten years, one that Nadya insisted be hidden in the larder, away from the reach of an angry hand or a thieving heart.

16

Sun Day, after noon

"Forgive?" Einar had asked. "How can you forgive the bad things people do?"

Sig remembered the first time Einar and the woman who was his new wife had argued, and he recalled the irony that Einar's first argument with Nadya was, according to Anna, the very same one that he used to have with Maria.

Nadya closed her eyes, as she always did when she was quoting the Bible.

"'How many times shall my brother sin against me, and I forgive him? Seven times? And Jesus said, no, not seven times, but seventy times seven.'"

That was enough for Einar to really lose his temper.

"Don't spout that nonsense at me!" he roared. "You don't even believe it yourself anymore. If you did, you'd still be living with that lunatic preacher and his flock of idiots! Forgive! Tell me, girl, how you would forgive a man who'd murdered you?"

"No one is going to murder us," Nadya said. "This is a peaceful place."

"What do you know of anything?" Einar said viciously. "What have you seen of the world?"

"I've seen some of it."

That was true. Sig had managed to glean enough about her life with the revivalist preacher and his community to know that. The preacher had taught abstinence from alcohol, from meat, and most of all from sex, but it turned out that he didn't seem to believe those laws applied to him. Nadya had left soon afterward, coming down from the Finnish border and ending up working at a hotel in Giron, which was where she'd met Einar.

"Then you should know there are evil men everywhere, and if one of them comes here one day while I'm away, you'll be glad I taught the boy to shoot!"

At that, Sig felt his heart start to race, but a moment later he heard the door slam as Anna stormed out of the cabin, unable to bear the fight between her father and her stepmother.

"Boy!" Wolff called through the wall.

Sig hurried back into the cramped space between the three doors, each leading to a different ending, a different path.

One path led outside, to running away.

One path led back inside, to Wolff.

And one path led back into the storeroom, to the Colt.

But if his path led there, wondered Sig, where in God's name would it go after that?

Sig paused in the hall, looking at his boots. He put the coffee tin down for a few moments while he pulled them on. He was not going outside, but something told him it might be a good idea to be ready.

"Sorry," he said, coming back into the cabin. "The first tin was almost empty. Full one."

He shook the tin at Wolff, the beans inside rattling noisily.

"Won't be long."

Sig turned to the counter that ran under the window by the back of the cabin, looking out into the pine forest. He pulled the coffee grinder from the shelf above the window, measured out a good handful into its feeder, and began to wind the little handle. The smell of the beans immediately filled the room, a reassuring smell that gave Sig no comfort now.

"Why the boots?" Wolff asked, almost casually.

God damn me, the man misses nothing, thought Sig.

"My . . . my feet were cold," he offered as an explanation. He hurried on before he could be challenged. "It's been a long, cold winter, everything frozen up, even the work at the Bergman mine was stopped when the winch gear stuck. The lake froze solid, and—"

"But not solid enough."

79

Wolff dropped the words onto the floor like little spiders, which scuttled over to Sig and crawled up his legs, his back, his neck. He stopped grinding the coffee briefly but then determined that he would not let the man rile him.

"I'm afraid so," he said simply.

Sig finished grinding the beans and took a mug down from the shelf. Opening the drawer of the grinder, he stuck a spoon into the lovely dark coffee grounds and lifted out a large rounded heap, placing it in the mug, as carefully as if it had been the gold dust his father used to weigh in Nome.

He poured the water onto the grounds, which floated to the top, then began to stir for a while, letting them settle to the bottom of the mug again. Warily he walked over to Wolff and handed him the drink.

Sig cursed himself. His hand was shaking.

"Still cold?" Wolff said, and smiled. Again, Sig felt sick.

Wolff sipped at the coffee in an almost laughable way, Sig thought, like an old lady sipping at her tea. He blew on it and took another sip.

"What?" Wolff said.

Sig shook his head.

"Sorry, nothing."

Wolff put down the mug.

"No. What do they mine?"

"Oh. Oh. Iron. They mine iron. It's an iron mine."

"Yes, I understand," Wolff said, his lips grinning but his eyes flat, unreadable.

"My father was the assayist."

"Yes," said Wolff. "Like in Nome."

"I suppose so. Yes."

"Only there," Wolff said, leaning forward in his chair, "it was something else we were mining, was it not?"

Sig nodded.

"My father says iron is a better thing to mine. He says—said—you can trust iron, that it's a reliable thing to mine, not like gold. Nobody gets killed over iron mining, that's what my father says."

Sig had been trying to lift the tone, to see if Wolff was actually not as frightening as he seemed, but he knew as soon as he'd uttered the words they'd been a mistake. Wolff just stared back at him, a gaze that stabbed, pinning him to the wall as if he'd been run through with a lance.

"And what would you know about that?" Wolff drawled.

"Nothing," Sig said. "Nothing. I only meant . . ."

He didn't finish his sentence because he couldn't think what to say.

"Yes," said Wolff. He took another sip of coffee. "Where the hell am I anyway? This town—Giron? No. Don't tell me, I don't want to know. I know I came through Finland. Is this still Finland? And before that was Russia.

My God! Russia. How big is that place? Do you have any idea how long it's taken me?"

Sig stood watching Wolff. He said nothing. He didn't think the man really wanted him to say anything, and his tongue had suddenly loosened.

"Yes, you do. I suppose you made that journey too. Ten years. It's taken me ten years to get here. But then I had a few false starts on the way . . ."

He looked around the cabin.

"Looks like it took you a few less. But then I didn't know where I was going. Always looking, always looking. For a man and two children. Here. There. Asking, always asking . . . But now I've found you. How long have you been here? Three years, I think. Yes. And do you know why I came?"

Sig shook his head.

"Do you know why I came?" Wolff repeated.

Still Sig said nothing.

"I think you know. I think you do. I had some business to attend to with your father."

Sig took a deep breath, and once more felt that strange detachment from what he was saying, as if he were observing this little scene from above.

"I'm very sorry your journey was wasted. But my father can't help you anymore, and you've had your coffee. You'll be needing to get back to Giron before dark. There's a hotel. It's quite good, I think. At the railway station."

82

He ran out of things to say, and Wolff stayed exactly where he was.

"I don't think you understand. Since your father is no longer with us, that makes you his heir.

"That means my business is with you."

17

Sun Day, after noon

"Your father and I had a deal. We worked together. Back in Nome. We had a deal. An arrangement of sorts. It seems that he'd forgotten. He left, without saying good-bye. I came here to remind him of our arrangement."

He made it sound like a casual thing, a chat over a glass of beer maybe. It didn't speak of ten years of what could only be an obsession.

"I'm sorry," said Sig. "I don't know anything about it. I would help you if I could. I'm sure you can see. I was only little at the time. It was—"

"Ten years ago. Yes. I know. It has taken me a whole damned decade to find you, and now . . . he dies the day before I arrive. But I think you might be able to help me. You were only a little boy then, but I'm sure you remember me."

Sig didn't.

He could remember so little of his time in Nome. He could remember the cold, colder even than Giron, and he could remember the emptiness of the place. He could remember Front Street, but he couldn't remember what their shack was like, just the odd scene, a moment here and there, frozen into his memory forever.

He could remember his mother barely at all, not even her face, and they hadn't had any photographs made that might now stimulate a recollection—of her gentle eyes perhaps, or the long, dark, wavy hair that Anna had inherited. No, nothing like that, but he could remember her as a feeling, a soft and warm feeling, making him safe and happy.

He could hardly remember what his father was like in those days. He'd had more hair then though, and one of Sig's few memories of Nome was of a particular habit of Einar's.

Sig remembered how he wore his hair, slicked back with oil, but only when he went to work. Every morning, he'd carefully stroke the oil into his hair so it was straight back and sleek as a raven's wing. He said it was to make him look more businesslike when he was weighing people's gold and paying out the dollars, so people took him more seriously. And every night he'd wash the oil out again in their little makeshift bathroom, so he looked like the father whom Anna and Sig knew and loved.

Even now, if Sig smelled the right kind of oil, it would

remind him of that early year of his life spent in Nome.

"I'm sorry," Sig said. "I don't remember you."

"No?" asked Wolff, raising an eyebrow. "No, perhaps not. But I do need to end this business that I spoke of. You understand?"

Wolff waited for some sort of reply, but didn't get one. He shrugged, as if to say, "Never mind."

Wolff stood, and for a moment Sig thought he might be leaving, but he merely arched his back, so hard that Sig heard all his vertebrae clack and snap back into place.

"Damn horse," he said, then sat down again. "Never mind. You don't remember me. But I'm sure your sister will. Now, when will she be home?"

18

Sun Day, dusk

"Father never mentioned you," Sig said. "Not to me, anyway. I don't suppose Anna will be able to help you much either."

He put the coffee grinder away and began to tidy the cabin, though in truth there was nothing out of place. It gave him an excuse not to look at Wolff's face, at those eyes that followed him everywhere. They were eyes which took a lot and gave nothing.

"That so?" Wolff said. He got up off his chair and involuntarily Sig backed away a little, but Wolff headed for the window.

"Getting dark. Your sister will be home before dark."

He turned to Sig.

"Lamp."

Sig did as he was told. He knew he should try to act as normally as he could. He bent to the stove and pulled out a burning taper, with which he lit the lamps hanging at either end of the room. Wolff stretched his legs a couple of times around the cabin table, his eyes mocking Einar's form under the blanket.

"Should bury him."

"I tried," said Sig. "Ground's too hard. The spade broke."

"Should bury him." It seemed to be something gentle from Wolff, but then he added, "Before he starts to stink."

Wolff sat down again, and as he did so, his leather greatcoat swung back, and now at last Sig had a full view of his gun. He knew what it was immediately, because it was the same as the one that waited in the box behind the coffee tins.

A Colt Single Action Army, the Frontier Six Shooter, though this one was clearly much newer than Einar's gun.

Wolff saw Sig's eyes linger briefly at his hip, and he smiled. He didn't bother to hide the gun, or the string of shiny brass cartridges held in a belt at his waist.

Sig turned but his mind had beaten him to it and was far away. It was his twelfth birthday. It was the spring before Einar had brought Nadya to live with them in the cabin, so it had just been the three of them: Einar, Anna, and Sig.

"Since it's your birthday," Einar had said, "you ought to have some kind of present."

At that, Anna and Sig had both paid attention. No one got presents. It simply didn't happen. They didn't have money for that kind of thing, but Einar had explained.

"This isn't the kind of present that you unwrap from a gift store. Though it does come in a box."

He chuckled, and his eyes shone.

"Sig, for your birthday, I'm going to show you the most beautiful thing in the world. Well, after your sister, and your dear mother, that is. The most beautiful thing in the world. Would you like that?"

Sig nodded.

"Yes," he said eagerly, then remembered his manners. "Yes, please."

Einar returned the nod solemnly.

"Very well. Then sit at the table, and shut your eyes. Wait there."

Sig sat down, and Anna crowded in at his elbow, delighted that her brother was going to have a present, though a small bit of her remembered that she'd never had one. The only toy she'd ever owned had been that doll, when she was little.

Still, her father was acting rather strangely, so when he returned carrying a box she hadn't seen in many years, she grew uneasy.

"There," Einar said, putting the box on the table. "You can open your eyes. Good. Inside this box is the most beautiful thing in the world."

Sig looked at the box. He couldn't remember having seen it before, though he had, and it stirred something within him, as if it were an old familiar friend.

"Go on. Lift the lid."

Sig didn't open the box immediately, but looked at it for a long time first, as if waiting for it to do something, or to speak to him in some way. It had a small catch, which finally he flicked to one side, and lifted the lid.

Inside was the gun.

"How is that the most beautiful thing in the world?" Anna said. "It's horrible. It's old and scratched and dirty, and anyway, it's a gun."

She got up from the table, and moved a pace or two away. Sig had to admit she had a point.

Einar shrugged.

"Well, it's old, that's true. Even when I bought the gun it was already old, an 1883 manufacture of the 1873 model. It's over twenty years old, now."

The blued finish of the metal, designed to protect the gun from rust, was wearing thin in places, scratched and pitted in others. The wooden grips had lost their varnish and been worn unevenly from frequent handling at some point in its early life.

Einar lifted the gun from the box, leaving behind all those things that Sig had wanted to touch when he was five years old, the cleaning tools, the disassembly tools, the oil, the wax. The cartridges.

It lay on the table like a beast, and already Sig began to feel what his father meant, he already sensed its power.

"Anna," said Einar. "Things are not only beautiful

90

from the way they look on the outside, like you. Things can also be beautiful from the inside, because of what they can do."

"But how is that beautiful on the inside?" she said, and despite herself, came closer to the table, lifting a strand of hair from her eyes and tucking it behind her ear.

Sig said nothing, just watched, listened, waited.

"Look," Einar said, picking it up again. "Look at this. It is a machine. It's a machine—perhaps a perfect one. We have machines at the mine, for drilling, for lifting, for sifting. They work, but they are all hideous, clanking, clunking mules. They break down all the time. The Colt is the finest machine I have ever seen in my life. It does one thing, and it does it superbly well. Look.

"Imagine I take one of those cartridges there, from the box. I'm not going to, but imagine I did. It's a tiny thing. But it's made from four separate parts. There's the case, the brass case that makes up most of its length. At one end, the back of the case, is the percussion cap, a small disc of copper with a little fulminate of mercury inside. At the other is the bullet itself, a tiny cone of lead weighing so very little. Inside the case is the gunpowder."

Anna's interest had started to wane again and she felt a little resentment sour inside her. There was always the risk of this, she suddenly realized, the bond between father and son, their mutual fascinations, the things they spoke about, always a step away from her.

Sig stared intently at the gun as his father spoke, trying to really see what he was merely describing.

"Imagine I took this cartridge, and lifted back the gate on the back of the cylinder here. It slides into one of the six chambers, a perfect fit. Everything measured and made to perfection. I pull back the hammer on the back of the gun, just halfway at first, so I can rotate the cylinder into place. Now the cartridge we loaded is sitting directly under the firing pin, on the underside of the hammer."

While Einar spoke, Sig gazed at the gun, and the gun alone. Einar pulled back the hammer to its full extent, which set into place with a tidy click, and now Anna couldn't help looking at the gun as well.

Suddenly there was a loud snap of metal. Einar had pulled the trigger. In truth it was only the crack of a hammer on a nail, but Sig jumped like a startled rabbit.

"If that had been loaded, you would have heard the bang at the other end of the lake. At least you would on a still day. And it's over before it's begun—that's how it seems when you pull the trigger. But if I told you what happened in that moment, you might not believe me."

"Tell me," said Sig, like that same rabbit bounding into a snare the hunter had set for it.

Einar smiled.

"You will have to use your imagination. Can you do that? Good. Well, when the hammer hits the percussion cap, the fulminate of mercury explodes, for it cannot tolerate being struck. You see? Once the cap explodes, it sets fire to the gunpowder inside the case, and instantly the temperature inside the case rises to a couple of thousand degrees, as hot as the smelting works at the mine, but all inside that tiny brass case.

"Now, Sig, the brass case, being so hot, there and then expands, and swells to press against the inside of the chamber, and so now it releases its grip on the lead bullet. This bullet is sitting at the front of the miniature fire in the case, with gases that expand and send it out of the chamber and off down the barrel. And this is the most remarkable thing of all. For the barrel down which the bullet must travel is, by a fraction, smaller than the bullet."

"But you said everything was measured to perfection."

"And so it is. Because inside that barrel is a series of three grooves, set out in a spiral down its length. The bullet, which is lead, and with the hellfire of that explosion behind it, is now both hot and soft. It's forced into those spirals. They bite into it, so that as it makes its way down the barrel, it spins. It spins and spins, and by the time it leaves the barrel, with the last of the gas pushing out behind it, it's not only spinning faster than Rumpelstiltskin, it's moving at over a thousand feet per second, which means that the bullet has hit whatever the barrel was pointing at before the bang has even left your ears.

93

"Perfection," Einar said. He paused, and Anna marveled at the look in his eyes, because it was one of love. "Do you see what I mean now? It's perfect, and if perfection is beauty, then this is the most beautiful thing in the world. A piece of man's incredible ingenuity, a machine, perfectly designed around the hand of man."

Einar put down the gun and with that same hand he reached to gently stroke Anna's cheek, but before he could, she recoiled.

Sig didn't say anything but studied the gun on the table where Einar had set it again.

Anna stood at his shoulder, her eyes clouding.

"But what happens when the bullet hits something?" she said. "Someone, I mean. That's not beautiful. That's terrible."

Einar scowled.

"Anna, for once . . . You sound like your mother. I'm just trying to explain . . ."

"What?" Anna said, her anger suddenly welling out of her. "If you're going to explain it to him, you should explain both halves of it, not just one!"

She grabbed the gun from the table.

She lifted it and pointed it at Sig's forehead, no more than a few inches away. All three knew the gun was not loaded, and yet the act was terrible.

"How does that feel?" she cried. "Does that feel beautiful, Sig?"

Einar got up angrily and left the table, left the cabin, left Anna's rage to dissipate, but before it did, Sig learned that having even an empty gun pointed at you is an awful thing. He could feel the muzzle pressing into his forehead like a strong thumb, though it was in fact inches away. He felt his lip twitch, and it occurred to him to wonder what in hell it would feel like if the gun were actually loaded.

Eventually, seeing his sister start to cry, he put his hand up and took the gun from her. It was the first time he had held it since that time in the shack in Nome, and now he had only a single emotion, no, not even that, merely a single thought.

The gun was heavy. He had forgotten how heavy it was.

Later that day, when everyone had calmed down, Einar had taken them out to the back of the cabin, by the woods, and let them each fire one shot, so that they knew how.

"We can't afford more than one for each of you," he said. "This is an old gun, and we only have the old ammunition left for it. They make the gunpowder smokeless now, and the smokeless is much more powerful. This old thing probably wouldn't stand it. Would blow it apart. Anna, you're oldest, you will have the first try."

There were eight cartridges left in the box.

He took two of them and loaded the first two cylinders, then handed the gun to Anna.

Einar let her take the weight of the gun with her own

strength. Anna looked at her father and he nodded back, reassuring her.

"There. Gently. Keep it steady. Pull the hammer back with your thumb. Use the sights, line them up on the tree you want to hit. When you pull the trigger keep it steady, hold your breath. Pull it fast or slow, it doesn't matter, just keep it steady. Now. When you're ready."

Anna's finger squeezed reluctantly in on the trigger, and suddenly there was a bang louder than any noise Anna or Sig had ever heard before. Birds flew squawking from the depths of the forest, and chasing after them, the echo of the gunshot came back across the lake.

"I missed," said Anna.

"No, you didn't," Einar said. "There, look at the tree."

There was a splintered hole the size of a fist in a pine thirty feet away.

"But I wasn't aiming for that one," Anna said. She laughed, and then they all laughed.

Sig took the gun from Anna, and now he, too, took aim. He felt the weight of the cold metal and found his mind blurring with everything Einar had said about what was to happen. He let all of it drift out of his head, and he looked down the sights.

A moment later, and it was all over again, just as Einar had said it would be.

His ears ringing from the bang, Sig heard Anna say, "He missed too!"

"No, he didn't," Einar said, a fat note of pride in his voice. "Look, he hit your hole. It's bigger. Is that what you were trying to do, son?"

Sig nodded.

He tried not to smile, for Anna's sake, but inside he felt the best he'd ever felt in his whole life. It had felt amazing, incredible, indescribable. It hadn't been frightening at all.

The only frightening thing was how easy it had been, but it would be years before he understood that.

19

Sun Day, dusk

If Wolff felt any discomfort at sharing a table with a dead man, he didn't show it.

"What food?" he'd said, and Sig had boiled up some palt, the local dish of meatballs in potato, from a pot that had gone cold the day before.

He swung his chair around so it sat at the end of the table, and when Sig brought the palt over, Wolff pushed Einar's feet to one side, making more than enough space for the bowl.

Sig watched and hated himself for not shouting at Wolff, for not telling him to stop being so disrespectful to his father, even though his father could take no more offence.

"You not eating?" Wolff said.

Sig shook his head.

Wolff shrugged and shoved Einar's booted legs farther out of the way.

"Just you stop that!" Sig blurted, before he knew what he was doing.

The spoon hung in the air, halfway to Wolff's mouth. Slowly it went down into the bowl again. Wolff stared ahead of him, his right side toward Sig, his coat back, the gun gleaming in its holster.

Before Sig could move, Wolff sprang from the chair, knocking it flying behind him, and with his hand on Sig's chest backed him against the rough cabin wall. He towered above Sig, breathing foul air over him. More than his breath, he stank of horse and sour sweat.

For a moment it seemed that Wolff would simply kill him, right there, but a moment passed, and then another, and, moving away slowly, Wolff picked up the chair and set it in front of the stew again.

He sat down, grabbed the spoon, and went on eating.

Sig slumped against the wall; he felt warmth trickle down his neck. Wolff had shoved him so hard he'd cut the back of his head.

"I'm hurt," Sig stated, feeling for the blood with his fingertips.

Wolff blew on his stew and slurped a mouthful.

"Is that my problem?"

It wasn't a question that expected an answer.

Sig said nothing. The cut wasn't too bad, and he had learned something. Terrified of Wolff's anger as he was, at least he had managed to rattle him, at least he had managed to make him angry, and that was better than facing the cold automaton he'd been up till then.

It made Sig feel less as if he were a fly waiting to be squashed by a boot, and more like a boy facing a giant.

20

Sun Day, dusk

"You like games?"

Sig put the empty bowl on the side by the window, wondering what Wolff was going to do next. In his mind he realized he had begun to plan distances and speeds, judging the route to the door, to the outside, to the storeroom. But every time he did, he pushed it away again. The gun was at the man's hip, for God's sake. He'd be dead before the last wisp of hot gas had left the barrel. Sig realized that the newer gun Wolff carried would use the latest smokeless powder Einar had told him about. Super-powerful and leaving barely a trace of evidence of the bullet that had killed Sig, it would throw his body across the cabin's floorboards with frightening ease.

"I said, do you like games?"

"We don't have time," Sig said, giving a truthful answer.

There had been days when he and Anna swam in the lake or played in the snow, but those days seemed to have curled up in the distance like a dying dog, never to return, though they'd found an amazing thing on their first winter in Giron. A trick of the snow, that they'd never seen before, despite having spent all their short lives in the far North.

They'd been exploring the short, scrubby trees behind the cabin, on the verge of the forest, and as Sig walked across the snow, it suddenly gave way, sending him crashing up to his waist.

From several paces behind, Anna laughed.

"Sig! I have you now!"

She scooped a snowball that she delivered right into Sig's face, and Sig, held fast by the deep snow, was unable to dodge it.

He cursed her and laughed at the same time, then called, "You try it! There's some kind of crust to the snow. These trees aren't really this short. They're up to their necks, too. Just like me!"

Anna saw what he meant and gingerly began to step across the snow after him. Her feet sank in only a few inches, and she was within a foot or so of Sig when she sped up—and immediately sank to her waist as well.

It was a peculiarity of snow falls, thaws, and refreezes, and it seemed to happen only every once in a while, when the weather was just right.

Later that day, finding a fresh patch to try, they lured Einar to the trees and laughed as his greater weight sent him floundering up to his chest almost immediately. Still laughing, they pounded him with snowballs.

"Well," said Wolff. "We have the chance for a little game this evening, don't we? It will pass the time till your sister gets home."

He moved the chair back from the table, swinging his legs to place his boots beside Einar's, poking out from the blanket, but this time he didn't touch the body.

"Here's how the game works. I will ask you a question. If you tell me the right answer, I will walk out of here, get my horse, and leave. If you don't tell me the right answer, I will stay here. And if you tell me an answer that is wrong . . ."

He smiled, and Sig thought he might finish the sentence, but he didn't bother. Sig didn't want to know, anyway, what awful thing the man would do to him.

"Are you ready to play? Good."

Sig stood by the window that looked at the lake and prayed that his sister would return, not alone, but with Nadya and some men from the mine. Mr. Bergman perhaps, or some of the younger men.

"So, here's my first question. Where is the gold your father stole from me?"

21

Sun Day, night

Can you feel something, see something, smell it, and touch it just by thinking about it?

As Sig wondered what he was going to say that wouldn't get him hurt, he found himself unable to concentrate on anything but the Colt. It was as if the gun were calling to him from the storeroom, and though it was ten feet away in a closed wooden box, Sig could feel the cold weight in his hand, smell the metal and oil and even the delicious waft of the burned powder after it had sent its little parcel of death spinning through the air toward Wolff.

It had sometimes puzzled Sig why a bullet did so much damage, how a small thing like that could kill so easily, even if it didn't hit your heart or your head, until Einar had explained how the enormous force held in the bullet rips open a cavity as large as a fist, maybe bigger, in whatever it hits. If the thing is flesh, then the cavity collapses again, but the damage has been done, and the loss of blood is great.

Sig stared at Wolff but didn't see him. All he saw were the sights of the Colt; the hammer at the rear, cocked and ready to fall on the cartridge, and the target sight at the tip of the barrel. It had been years since he had held the gun, but it was all still crystal clear in his mind.

Wolff was waiting for an answer to his question. He leaned back in his chair, and there was his own revolver again, lurking in the hip holster. Wolff let his hand drop toward the gun, making an obvious show of it. His hand reached the butt and his fingers tickled the backstrap and hammer, but he left it where it was.

His eyes bored right through Sig. He didn't have long.

"Would you like some more coffee?" Sig stumbled out.

Wolff paused before answering, and when he did, merely nodded.

Sig held his breath, trying to steady himself.

"G-good," he stuttered. "I mean, I'll get some."

He turned for the door out to the hallway and the storeroom, and even as he did, he realized his mistake.

"Wait!"

Wolff barked the command, stopping Sig in his tracks. "The coffee's already in here, boy. Over there, on the side." Then he spoke more quietly, the words curdling in his throat. "Where you left it."

Sig turned quickly back into the room, trying to hide his guilt.

"Yes, I forgot. Yes."

He began to fumble some more water into the kettle, slopping it onto the stovetop, sending a hiss of steam into the cabin. He turned to the coffee grinder, and was almost relieved when Wolff spoke.

"Forget the coffee. Answer the question."

Sig turned back to Wolff.

"I'm sorry. My father has no gold."

Wolff stood up.

"I'm only going to ask this question three times," he said. "Second time. Where is the gold your father stole from me?"

Now the words tumbled out of Sig.

"Please," he said rapidly. "I don't know anything about it. My father doesn't have any gold. I've never seen any. We've never been rich; we've always been moving till we came here. We never had anything, or stopped anywhere for long, until we came here. I don't know anything about anything. We don't have any gold."

"You had enough money to buy this place."

"No," Sig said. "The Company owns it. Bergman's Mining. They own everything."

"That may be true, or it may not," Wolff said, "but the fact remains that your father owes me a lot of money. In gold. That he stole from me. We had an arrangement."

"What arrangement?"

Wolff took a step towards Sig.

"That's between him and me. And he's dead." Wolff smiled, yellow teeth showing behind the ragged ginger beard, and then said, "Though even the dead tell stories."

"What did you say?" Sig asked incredulously.

"What?" Wolff grunted.

"That was one of my father's sayings," Sig stated flatly, as if it had been stolen.

Wolff grinned, remembering.

"Yes. It was. Even the dead tell stories. But it seems to be another mistake your father made. He's saying nothing, I think. So now, you had better do his storytelling for him. I've followed him for ten years, wanting to hear how the story ends.

"I've nearly frozen to death. Twice. I have starved. I have eaten things no man should eat. I've crawled through the snow and the ice and damn near lost my other thumb to frostbite like I lost my first. And a man without thumbs is nothing. I could have laid down and died a thousand times over the last ten years, but I didn't. I kept going, because all the time, I knew my gold was waiting for me.

"And now I am here, and I have asked the question twice, so I will ask it one more time, and you will tell me the answer."

He took another couple of steps toward Sig, who

107

backed away, and felt his heels kick the wall. Nowhere else to go.

Wolff thrust his neck out and pushed his head and his mad eyes right into Sig's face.

"Where," he whispered, with a voice as from a slit throat, "is the gold your father stole from me?"

Sig closed his eyes. It wouldn't be long now. He only had to be brave while it happened.

He took a breath.

He spoke slowly, so slowly, and gently, as if speaking to a young child on a summer's day.

Each word became a sentence.

"I. Don't. Know."

There was an infinitesimal pause, a tiny gap of space and time in which Sig felt his heart stop beating, and then Wolff shoved Sig's head against the wall, reopening the cut from earlier.

Sig howled and dropped to the floor. His eyes swam from the pain and he crouched on all fours. In the corner of his vision, he could see Wolff's boots, saw one swing back, ready to aim a kick at his head.

Then there was a stamp of footsteps on the porch outside, and moments later, a fumbling at the latch.

The swinging boot stopped midway, and Sig tilted his head to the door, like a dog waiting for his master to come home.

The door opened.

Anna came in.

As Sig pulled himself to sit against the cabin wall, Wolff's eyes ran all over Anna, from her snowy feet to the last strand of her long and wavy brown hair, falling in places from underneath her fur hat, to her rosy cheeks, flushed from the cold, and ended on her round young lips.

"Well." The words slipped from his mouth and crawled over her. "Haven't you grown?"

Sig strained to see past Anna, then hung his head.

She was alone.

Even God leaves on the last boat from Nome.

ANON

1900

Nome

66 LATITUDE NORTH

22

The Rim of the World

For the newborn population of Nome there was a little joke they liked to quote at each other all the time. They would say, "There are only two seasons in Nome, Winter and the Fourth of July." Einar and Maria shared the joke, though they knew the reality that lay behind the casual words.

But by the time the Fourth of July came around, things were good for Einar and his family. Maria's illness and the horrors of the long grim winter of almost perpetual night had been forgotten. Einar had put the Colt back in its box and hid it out of sight of the children, as Maria wished.

Maria would stay at home with her son and daughter during the day, gradually turning the shack into a place fit to live in, getting them to help with a little simple cooking and cleaning, or she'd go shopping and nod a greeting to the other few respectable ladies who'd arrived now.

115

The town itself was improving. A pipe was built to run from the creek in the hills right down Front Street, so everyone there could get clean fresh water with ease. The saloon was finished—the first two-story building in town, with twelve rooms upstairs and none of them for whores.

There was a rustle of gossip around the town one day, as news leaked out that there was a new co-owner of the saloon, no less than the infamous gunslinger Wyatt Earp, who'd bought a stake in the bar and would soon be arriving by ship.

And Einar was working, bringing in if not a fortune, then certainly enough money to clothe and feed his family, with some to spare if they were careful.

He'd been working at the Assay Office for a few months and was doing well. Mr. Salisbury made a visit every now and again to see how he was getting on, and each time said he was very pleased with Einar's work.

"You've had no trouble learning the chemistry, Einar?" Mr. Salisbury asked.

Einar shook his head.

"No, sir," he said truthfully. "I've always had the kind of mind that likes to know things. Things about the world, about how things work. Do you know what I mean, sir?"

Mr. Salisbury laughed.

"Yes, I do. But there's not many people who do, it seems to me. Good for you, Einar. Keep learning and there'll always be work for a man like you."

He leaned in close so that no one else in the Assay Office could hear.

"The truth of it? You want to know the truth? None of these miners, the prospectors, are ever going to be rich. Most of them will keep finding just enough gold dust to make them think their dreams are around the corner, but they will never come. Some will even find a strike, and be rich for a few days till they blow it all. And the only people who are actually going to get rich are you and me, the people in the town running businesses. Like Mr. Earp with his saloon, when he gets here.

"So don't fall for the lure of gold again, Einar. That's the truth of it."

Mr. Salisbury left, and at the end of the day, Einar was closing up the office.

He shuffled out through the door, turning to lock it, and when he turned again he bumped straight into someone.

"Excuse me," he said, and then realized it was the bear-man. His name was Wolff, he'd learned, and he'd also learned that he was trouble.

"Got some to test," Wolff muttered.

"I'm very sorry, you'll have to come back in the morning," Einar said. "The office has closed for the day."

Einar tried to go on his way.

"So open it," Wolff said, not moving.

"I can't do that."

"Yes, you can. You have the key. You just locked it, you can open it again."

Einar felt his throat go dry.

"I'm very sorry. Mr. Salisbury is strict about things like that. I'd open it for you, but I'd be in a lot of trouble, you see. We don't want trouble."

Suddenly Einar found himself pressed against the glass of the door.

"No," Wolff said. "We don't want trouble. So open the door and test my gold."

"First thing in the morning, I promise."

"Can't do that. Have to get back to my claim tonight, in case someone jumps it. So I need it tested now."

Einar thought the chances of anyone trying to steal Wolff's claim from him were pretty slim, but he didn't say that. Still, he refused to be bullied by the man.

"I'm very sorry," he said slowly.

"You will be."

Einar saw the glint of a blade coming out of Wolff's pocket.

"You okay there, Einar?"

A voice called from the street.

Einar peered over Wolff's shoulder to see four of the regulars from the saloon watching the altercation.

"You okay? Need any help?"

Einar said nothing, but watched as Wolff's knife slid back into his pocket.

Wolff turned.

"He's fine," he said, and slunk away down the street.

"Okay, Einar?" called his friends. "Coming for a drink?"

"No. Thanks. No, I think I'd better get home. Supper on the table, you know how it is!"

"Sure do, you lucky man!"

His friends left, and Einar hurried the other way up the street, heading for home, while his friends congratulated Einar on having such a beautiful wife, even if she did quote the Bible too often for their comfort.

Standing on a porch two buildings away, Wolff watched him go.

23

The Book of Job

Even the dead tell stories. Einar had inherited the saying not from his Swedish father, but from his mother. It was a proverb that meant, as far as the young Anna could work out, nothing is ever truly finished; the past is always with us.

She worked it out for herself, as she worked out many things for herself that summer while Einar toiled in the Assay Office and Maria tried to turn a hut into a home.

There was a saying of Maria's, too, which Anna learned quickly, because her mother said it often: "Let's not speak of the snow that fell last year." Anna noticed her mother said it when people were arguing over something that had happened a while ago.

Mr. Salisbury heard her say it one day and decided to teach her the English version.

"Let bygones be bygones," he said carefully, playing the

schoolmaster, but Maria had laughed when she tried the words herself.

"I'll stick with what my mother said. *'Tala inte om den snö som föll i fjol.'* It sounds better."

It was around then Anna noticed something else about her mother. She noticed Maria quoted the Bible constantly, at every waking moment there would be something to learn from the Bible that Maria kept, stored preciously in a box, the same way Einar kept his Colt 44-40. The only difference was that one was out all the time, the other hidden. But waiting for its moment.

When Sig argued with Anna, which was rarely, Maria would admonish them both with "turn the other cheek." And if Sig was naughty or cross, she would tell him gently "turn from evil and do good."

The inhabitants of Nome had no church as yet, and the joke started to spread that Maria *was* the church. You only had to spend half an hour in her company to get a year's worth of preaching—that was what they said. And though Einar was a God-fearing man, Anna more than once heard her father question Maria's faith, though it was little Sig who really said something bad.

"If God loves us so much," he said, "why are we hungry so much?"

It was true that they were doing better than through

the dark winter when Maria was ill, but there were many days when they would go short of food. It was the way of Nome.

Maria sat down with Sig and explained it all to him. He sat on her lap and looked at the red flowers embroidered on her blue dress while she told him a story, from the Bible about a man called Job. It was a long and confusing story, and Anna, hanging around to listen, didn't follow it all that well.

Job was a good man who loved God, and who, no matter what bad things happened to him, refused to curse God's name and kept worshiping him. He lost his house and his servants and his family and all his sons and daughters, and still he kept believing in God's love.

Sig listened thoughtfully till his mother had finished speaking, and then said, "But why are we hungry all the time?"

Just then, Einar had walked in the door, home from the office. His hair was slicked back as usual, but before even going to wash out the oil, he swooped Sig up in his arms and made him a promise.

"We won't be hungry ever again, I promise. Not once we leave this town."

"Are we leaving, Einar?" Maria said, hope rising in her voice.

"We'll leave in the autumn. On the last boat. I'm going

to work the summer. But I promise we'll never spend another winter here."

And in their different ways, none of them would.

24

The Water That Burns

Though Einar had expected trouble from Wolff the day after he'd refused to reopen the office, the trouble never came.

Wolff had spent the night at the saloon and seemed perfectly civilized the next morning.

Nonetheless, he was first in the queue to have his gold tested and was waiting at the door of the office. Einar worked with two other men, also appointed by Mr. Salisbury, and who'd arrived on the first boat that summer. They were a frail old man called Wells, who worked as the clerk, and a man of Einar's age called Figges, who was a little slow but big. He seemed to be there to provide muscle in case of trouble.

The beauty of the relationship among the three of them, Einar soon realized, was that none of them trusted the other. Mr. Wells would scrutinize his record books, scratching away with a brass nib pen, but all the while he'd keep one eye twisted toward Einar. Einar went about his work methodically, and all the while kept his eye on Figges, who looked like a murderer who just hadn't found anyone to murder yet.

Figges sat at his desk, eating most of the day, his lazy eyes sloping from one of them to the other, and then back again.

But it was Einar who did all the testing and weighing. It was Mr. Salisbury himself who'd taught Einar how to use the fierce little crucible to smelt the gold, and the aqua fortis to remove impurities. Einar's table was a miniature laboratory, with a pair of balance scales, burners, and bottles of acid and other chemicals.

Wolff held out his tiny paper wrap containing some grains of gold to Einar.

"Test it."

"Would you like to come back? It can take a little—"

"I'll wait," Wolff said, and pulled over a chair to sit within a few feet of Einar.

Figges sat more upright in his chair, sensing trouble at last, and Wells kept scribbling and watching, all at once.

Unsettled, Einar set to work on Wolff's samples and prayed they were of high quality, not wanting to have to tell him his find was worthless.

His hands trembled as he got the burners going underneath the crucible, and Wolff saw.

"Cold?" he sneered. It was as hot a day outside as Nome had ever seen.

Einar ignored him and, dropping the small grains into the crucible, waited for the heat to do its work, running his hands nervously through his hair as he did, smoothing it till it was as sleek and black as a raven's wing.

While he waited, Einar began to prepare his acid, but his hands began to shake even worse as he saw Figges fingering a gun underneath his desk, eager for something to start.

Einar poured the aqua fortis and his hands betrayed him. He felt the nitric acid trickle onto his skin, and without thinking, he dropped the lot and ran to the sink.

"Thank God they built that pipe from the creek," he said over his shoulder, washing the acid off his hand, and washing it again until he was sure it was all gone. He'd moved fast and the burn wasn't too deep. With luck he might get away with no scarring, in time.

Wells peered over his rickety desk, Figges sat down again, but Einar saw that Wolff had seen the gun in Figges's paw.

Well, that might help in a way. Let Figges get killed. Einar had no interest in dying.

Einar dried his hands and, returning to his desk, picked up the bottle of acid and the funnel and cleaned everything twice. Fortunately his acid spill had missed the crucible, which was nearly done smelting the gold.

Einar prepared the acid, taking extra care, and dropped the remains from the crucible into it.

After a short wait, he drained and washed the tiny button of gold, then placed it on the scales.

His heart sank, and his eyes raised to Wolff as he gave the verdict.

"I'm sorry to say your sample is of ten percent purity at best. No more. Probably not worth the effort of digging it up."

He held Wolff's eyes, waiting for him to explode, but he didn't.

"Do you want cash for this?" Einar asked, proffering the tiny nugget toward Wolff.

"No," Wolff said, taking the gold back. "Not if it's worth so little. I'll keep it as a reminder."

Einar had no idea what he meant, but he breathed a sigh of relief that it was over.

Except it wasn't quite over.

Wolff stared at him for a long time, stared at him, absorbing every detail of his clothes and hair and face, his eyes burning through Einar's head like the acid had burned his hand.

He turned his gaze briefly towards Wells, then Figges for a little longer.

127

He took the chair he'd been sitting on, rested it against the wall, then sat down on it.

"Gentlemen," he said. "I find this whole business fascinating. You don't mind if I stay awhile. And watch."

25

The Hunter's Response

"We have to close now."

Einar stood behind his desk and tried to show Wolff that he wouldn't be intimidated.

Wells was folding up his spectacles and sliding them into a metal tube that served as a case. Figges had already left, bored of waiting for any possible trouble brewing.

All day Wolff had sat on the hard wooden chair till they'd almost forgotten he was there. Occasionally he would shift a leg or stretch, but otherwise, he sat, watching every move Einar made.

They'd had a steady stream of customers, and Einar had been busy, not even stopping for lunch. Wolff took no lunch either, and at the end of the day, Einar was glad to see him stand up the first time he asked. Some of the men had had good gold, others almost worthless. Wolff had watched them all just the same, watched Einar test their gold, weigh their grains, count out cash.

"Fascinating," he said. "Fascinating."

He left.

But the next day, as Einar had been working at his table for a couple of hours, he suddenly sensed that he was being watched through the window. He looked up to see Wolff staring at him. Immediately, the bear-man moved off down the boardwalk, but he came again the next day, and the next, and the next.

Finally, the day came when, five minutes before closing time, Wolff stood in front of Einar's table once more.

Wells and Figges were well used to the sight of Wolff now and made their way out of the office on the stroke of six with better things to do.

"I'm sorry," Einar said. "We're closing."

But he already knew that wasn't going to help him.

"I'm not here to have my gold tested. I'm here to make you a proposition."

Einar packed away his things, pretending not to hear.

"I said, I'm here to make you a proposition. A deal. An arrangement."

He came around to Einar's side of the table and looked at the materials, the equipment. He picked up a bottle of aqua fortis and shushed it gently around inside the bottle.

Einar grabbed it from him and set it back down softly on the table.

"What is it you want to say?"

Wolff smiled.

"I want half."

"I don't understand."

"I want half. I want half of your gold. You're a very clever man. You can understand that. Half."

"I don't know what you're talking about," Einar said. He continued to tidy things that didn't need tidying, till Wolff lost his patience and slammed Einar against the wall.

"Don't play with me. You might have deceived those idiots you work with, but you don't deceive me. I want half. I know how you do it. I want half, and in return, I keep my silence. Yes? A partnership. We are partners."

"Listen. Wolff," Einar said, wrestling free from Wolff's grip. "I don't know what you're talking about. If you think I'm stealing gold, you can see that it's just not possible. There's Wells and Figges, and everything is measured, weighed, recorded. Mr. Salisbury checks it every week. You've seen it all. You've seen it for yourself."

Wolff turned for the door.

"Good," he said. "Yes, I've seen it all. And now we are partners, Andersson. You understand that. It's a good arrangement, because we both get something from it. And I know I can trust you."

"You do?" Einar blurted out, not thinking.

"Yes," growled Wolff. "I do. Give my regards to your beautiful wife. And your sweet children."

131

The door swung shut behind him, and Einar sank into his office chair once more. He put his head in his hands, and he wept.

26

The Sound of the Sky

"Are we really leaving?" Anna asked her father one day at bedtime.

Einar smiled at Anna.

"Yes."

"But when? Before it gets cold again?"

"We'll leave on the last boat of the year," Einar said, stroking his daughter's wavy brown hair. Sig was snuffling away at the foot of his parents' bed, across the room. Maria was cleaning dishes and singing quietly to herself.

"But it will be cold by then, won't it, Pappa? Can't we leave before it gets cold again?"

"Don't you like the snow?" Einar asked. "The Northern Lights; the sounds they make?"

"Yes, but it just goes on and on and on. And it's so cold. Too cold. I didn't like it here last winter."

"No. And your mother was ill, but she's fine now, thanks to God for that. But I have to work as long as possible, so we need to stay till the last boat comes."

Anna considered this for a while, stroking the hair of her little wooden doll just as her father stroked hers. Then a frown crossed her face.

"Pappa?"

"What is it, little one?"

"I heard some men talking today. They said something funny. They said, 'Even God leaves on the last boat from Nome.' What does that mean?"

Einar's face stiffened briefly.

"They just mean things are a bit tough here in the winter," he said quietly, so Maria wouldn't hear. "But we know that. That's why we're leaving."

"Oh," said Anna, very sleepily. Her eyelids began to droop, but still she wanted to ask something else.

"Pappa? Are you friends with the bear-man?"

27

Avalanche

Apart from the scene with Wolff, things were going well for the Andersson family, and none of them, not even Einar, sensed the storm that was coming.

Maria sang every day, and Anna started singing with her. Sig seemed to grow an inch every month, and he loved the town, which seemed to get bigger every day, with new houses and shops going up all the time. Boats would come and go, bringing with them more people, more goods, more equipment, more horses, more dogs for when the winter came.

The place was a heaving mass, and Sig would run here and there whenever he got the chance, marveling at the sights, though Maria was always telling him not to go off by himself. He'd watch the loading and unloading of boats; the building of houses, shacks, and huts; and above all, the people, each carrying a bundle of stories inside them.

The brief summer was over, not quite in one day as the saying had it, but not so very much longer than that. There was no autumn. Then winter was back, not hard at first, but with every gust of wind came the smell of the snow to come.

It wouldn't be long before the last boat sailed.

On the day it happened, Einar was at work as usual. It was a filthy cold day, with angry gray skies of low clouds scudding fast across the heavens, so that even God didn't see what happened in the shack that had become the Anderssons' home.

Maria had her hands covered in flour and pastry when she suddenly realized Sig had sneaked out to play by himself again.

"Anna," she said. "I thought you were watching him. You'll have to go and find him."

Anna looked up from playing with her doll.

"Oh, but it's cold outside."

"I know it is, but that's all the more reason why you should have kept an eye on him. Go on, now. By the time you get back, Pappa will be home and supper will be ready."

Anna sighed as only a child can sigh and left her doll on the big bed.

"I'll be back soon," she said to it, playing mother. "Now, don't do anything naughty while I'm gone."

She slipped out of the door pulling her coat and gloves on as she went.

"Hurry, Anna!" called her mother.

Anna did hurry. She ran down Front Street toward the beach and the comings and goings of boats, because she knew Sig loved to watch. But he wasn't there.

So she tried back up behind Front Street, then over to the edge of town, toward the rows of miners' tents along the shore, the rising and falling pump arms, and way beyond that, the tents of the local people. Even at this distance she could hear their dogs barking, occasionally answered by a dog from town.

He wouldn't have gone that far, she thought. She hoped not, or her supper would be cold.

Then she had an idea. Maybe he'd gone to see Pappa at work. He wasn't supposed to, but he'd done it more than once.

Anna decided she'd try there, but when she met Einar, he hadn't seen Sig either.

She began to panic slightly, as she and her father hurried home. But he reassured her; they would get Maria and then they could all look.

They needn't have worried.

As they came up along Front Street once more, they saw Sig at last, though for some reason, he was standing in the doorway of the cabin, the door wide open, not going in.

Surely Maria would tell him to keep the cold out.

Einar walked a little faster, then faster still.

Then he ran, and Anna could not keep up.

She saw Einar reach Sig in the doorway, and then he froze as motionless as his son, both of them staring inside.

Suddenly Einar was shoving Sig backward, and as Anna arrived, he turned and shouted at her.

"Anna!"

He screamed at her.

"Anna! Take your brother away."

Anna didn't understand, and came closer.

"Anna," Einar screamed again. "Get away! Take Sig and get away!"

He thrust Sig into his sister's arms, and automatically she wrapped her arms around him.

"What is it, Sig?" she asked. "What's happened?"

She saw her father scramble into the room as if his legs had stopped working, and despite everything he'd said to her, she stumbled in a step after him.

She saw her mother, or most of her, lying on the floor. Her head was out of sight around the foot of the bed, but she was lying still and her legs stuck out at a strange angle. Her dress was rucked up above her knees, and then Anna saw the floor of the shack was slowly changing color, from brown to red.

It took her a moment to realize that it was a pool of

blood, but she was not a stupid girl, and in another moment she knew their mother was dead.

Lying in the middle of the pool of blood was Anna's doll.

A strong body makes the mind strong. As to the species of exercises, I advise the gun. While this gives moderate exercise to the body, it gives boldness, enterprise and independence to the mind. Let your gun therefore be the constant companion of your walks.

THOMAS JEFFERSON.
THIRD PRESIDENT OF THE UNITED STATES,
PRINCIPAL AUTHOR OF THE DECLARATION
OF INDEPENDENCE

1910

Giron

68 LATITUDE NORTH

28

Sun Day, night

"I thought you weren't coming." Wolff grinned at Anna.
Anna stared at him for a fraction of a second, her
eyes flicked to Sig for some explanation.

"But here you are," Wolff continued, drawing back
slightly. "Did you bring your dogs back? You are very
quiet."

Anna ignored Wolff and stepped toward Sig to help
him up.

"Are you all right?"

Sig nodded.

"What's going on?" she whispered, but a single look
from Sig was enough to tell her that it was bad.

Anna helped Sig to a chair, and then she noticed his
head.

"You're bleeding!"

"It's fine," Sig said, gingerly feeling the cut on the back
of his skull.

145

"No, it's not," Anna said, and went to get some water and a cloth. As she did, she kept one eye on the stranger in the house.

Wolff sat down again opposite Sig, bringing a chair over from the table.

"Well," he said. "Isn't this cosy? A nice family scene. Though your family has just got smaller, hasn't it?"

Anna glared at the stranger.

"Do I know you? Have we met?"

Sig waved a hand at Wolff.

"This is Mr.—"

"Gunther Wolff, at your service."

Sig stared at Wolff. Was he trying to be charming now? A moment before, he had been ready to kill him, or as good as.

"He says he knew Father. Ten years ago. He says—"

"Yes," said Anna. The color drained from her face. "Yes, I remember you."

29

Sun Day, night

"Will you sit?"

Wolff inclined his head toward a third chair, still sitting by the table on which Einar lay.

Reluctantly, Anna took the chair and moved it near to where Sig was sitting.

"Yes, just the two of you now," Wolff said.

"Three," said Sig. Anna shushed him, but it was too late.

"Three?" Wolff said, sitting up. "Is there another child? No, because you have no mother. So . . ."

"There's Nadya," said Sig. "She's our mother now."

"Sig, be quiet," Anna said.

Wolff watched the exchange with amusement.

"Where is she, anyway?" Sig asked Anna. "Didn't you get anyone to help?"

Anna said nothing but glared at Sig, who suddenly realized the danger of what he was asking.

Wolff clapped his hands.

"No one's coming to help? And this Nadya, your father's new woman, she's run off at the first sign of trouble, has she?"

"No!" said Sig, but Anna was silent.

"Tell him, Anna," said Sig.

"Stop being so stupid," Anna hissed, and Sig sat back as if he'd been slapped.

"You can't blame her," Wolff said casually. "She's lost her husband, her only chance of a little money and a good time, yes? She doesn't want to stick around to put up with you two. Off to find someone else, yes? Only sad thing is she obviously didn't know that your father is a wealthy man . . ."

Despite her revulsion at Wolff, Anna couldn't help her curiosity.

"Father didn't have money."

"Oh, don't you try that with me," Wolff said. "Because I won't have you lie to me."

"I'm not lying," Anna said.

"He says he had a lot of gold in Nome. He says Father stole it from him."

"Be quiet, boy!" Wolff snapped. "Your father had the gold, believe me. And he and I had a deal that he would give me half of it. I never got my half. I want it now."

"Father had no gold," Anna said. "We left Nome as poor as we are now. Can't you see with your own eyes? If

148

we'd been rich, do you think we'd have ended up living in this place?"

That seemed to throw Wolff.

"Don't lie to me," he said eventually. "Because I don't like it when people try to make a fool of me."

He rose and crossed the room toward where they sat. Defensively, Anna got to her feet and stuck out her chin.

Wolff moved up to her, towering over her though she was a tall young woman. He smiled at her and lowered his face to within a few inches of hers.

She blundered into the chair, knocking it over, and Wolff closed in on her, feeling for a lock of her tumbling hair, bringing it toward his mouth, smelling it. Then he kissed it.

Anna flinched and Wolff let her go.

Sig clutched the arms of his chair and stood so suddenly that Wolff spun to meet him.

Before he could blink, the revolver was in Wolff's hand and aiming at Sig's heart. The tip of the barrel was resting gently on his chest, digging into the cloth.

"Wait!" cried Anna.

Wolff turned his head lazily toward her.

"No. You listen to me. Both of you. I have to make a decision. Sit back down where you both were. Right now."

Sig stood, breathing hard, and now a moment had come that somehow he had been waiting years for.

Finally, he knew what it felt like to have a loaded gun pointed straight at you.

Anna stole a brief look at Sig, then picked up the fallen chair. They did as they were told and sat down. Sig could not stop staring at Wolff's revolver. It was much newer than his father's, but it was unmistakably the same gun, the 44-40, designed for ease of use to take the same ammunition as a Winchester rifle.

"Good," said Wolff, and he sat back down in his own chair. The Colt stayed dead still in his hand, lined up on the space between Sig and Anna.

"Now, I need to explain something to you. I just have to decide something, but before I do, let me explain.

"I know your father. I knew your father well. I have tracked him for ten years. Followed you all. You had a head start, it's true. He was a clever man. After your mother died, he told me he was leaving on the last boat. I reminded him about our agreement, and told him I'd be leaving on that last boat too. He knew that anyway.

"And he worked hard. There was about a month to go till that last boat came, and he worked every hour God sent. He even convinced Mr. Salisbury to keep the office open longer, so more miners could make their claims. Mr. Salisbury said what a good worker he was. So he worked and he worked, and the winter came, and the snows came, and just as the first ice started to form, that last boat came, headed for Seattle.

"The night before it sailed, we met in the saloon to conclude our deal. We met upstairs in one of the private rooms. Wouldn't do to see that much gold changing hands, Einar said. He was right. We had a drink to celebrate. Einar had brought some whisky and we drank. He was very nervous. I guessed it was because he thought he was getting off without me blowing his game wide open. He'd have been in jail for a long time, and you two with no mother. But if I'd done that, I'd never have got my gold. So the deal had worked pretty well.

"We had another drink, and then, all of a sudden, I was sick. Sick as a dog. Your father was pretty good about it. Very nice of him. Gave me another glass of whisky. I sunk it straight off, and then the room started to spin, and I went down on the floor.

"Last thing I heard was your father saying good-bye. Said he had a boat to catch."

Wolff paused and his eyes flicked back to Sig and Anna, but they hadn't moved. Wolff's eyes narrowed.

"Your father was a devious bastard, I'll say that much for him." Wolff made it sound like a good and honorable thing.

"Yes. When I woke next morning it was late. I was still bad, really sick, but I made it to the beach to see that boat steam over the horizon. That pig from the Assay, Figges, told me you were aboard."

Anna looked at Sig, and Sig looked at Anna.

151

Wolff saw the look and grinned.

"Yes, you know it, but it took me a lot longer to work out exactly what he did. But you may not know how your father had rented the room in the saloon, so I wouldn't be found till morning.

"Or how, when I went to the doctor on Front Street, he told me I'd been poisoned. Not enough to kill me, just enough to knock me out. Forgot what the name of the stuff was, but the doctor told me it was something used in the testing of gold.

"And then your father's final trick, which you already know. I waited seven months in that frozen dump for the next boat to Seattle, and I took it, and when I got to Seattle I checked the passenger lists. What did I find? You'd never been on that boat at all. You can tell me now, since we're old friends. You didn't take that boat south. What did you do? Take a dog team someplace? East into Canada?"

Anna shook her head, and she felt a small victory her father had won, many years before.

"He'd bought a dog team from the Esquimaux camp. We headed west, to the farthest tip of Alaska. We made it across the ice to an island in the strait. Then we got lucky, and got a ride on a fishing boat heading for Russia."

Wolff shook his head. He stared at the body under the blanket for a while.

"He took two children across the ice on a dog sled? And you all made it?"

152

Anna was silent. She held her head a little higher, remembering the flight they'd made, traveling so light; a bundle of blankets, a Bible, a thin, flat box.

"So, you had seven months' head start, and I was on the other side of the Atlantic, on the other side of America. I guess he thought he'd never see me again. Or maybe he did, because yesterday I wound up in that two-bit little mining town across the lake.

"Before I got caught up in the gold craze, I was a hunter. I know how to track. Some tracks are left in the snow, others in people's memories, others in record books. It was a different kind of hunting, but I did it in the end. I had to go back to Nome to start off. First thing I did was blow a hole in Figges's head."

Wolff paused, obviously remembering the scene. He spat on the floor as though he had a bad taste in his mouth.

"Now and again I'd hear stories of a man and his two children, and then I began to close in on you, but maybe he'd get wind of me too, and then you'd disappear. I guess he thought he'd lost me forever. Maybe he was tired of running. Whatever. But when I got to this dump, I think Einar knew I was coming.

"He must have had a tip-off. Seen me in the street before I saw him. Asked people to keep an eye out for strangers, perhaps. Because when I went to his office he'd taken all his things, his papers, everything, like he was never coming back. Emptied out his safe. No one had seen him, though I asked all around town.

"Seems he set off home, ready to run again, and then the damn fool falls through the ice and freezes to death."

He paused.

"Quite a story, isn't it? But like I said, I am just explaining all this to you so you don't think I'm stupid. I know about your father, and the gold, and now I want it. Not just half of it. I want it all."

Sig shifted nervously in his chair. His memories of their journeying were faint, but for Anna, it was different. It made sense now. Why they'd run almost all their lives, and what it was Einar had been running from, what he'd been scared of. It was like hearing the other half of a story that had been hidden from her. All that time, Einar had been waiting for Wolff to track him down.

She swallowed her fear, and suddenly feeling the need for some kind of help, wondered where her mother's little black book was. Without knowing it she longed for the faith it contained, for the hope it might give, where there was none.

"Do you know the Bible?" she asked Wolff fiercely. "I doubt you do, but there's a story in there about a man called Job. And how, no matter what bad things happened, he didn't stop believing in God's love."

Wolff raised an eyebrow and leaned closer to Anna.

"What of it, my sweet?"

"Well, Sig and I are like that. It doesn't matter what you do to us, or what bad things happen. We won't stop believing in each other. Do you see?"

Wolff sneered at her.

"Is that so? Well, this may surprise you, but I did my time in church too. I know that story, and I know what most people who quote it seem to like to forget. It wasn't Satan who tortured Job. It was God. God and Satan made a bet, to test him, to see if he would crumble. Lose his faith. And then, without mercy, they piled misery on him, again and again and again. So, if there is a God up there, you can bet your worthless little life he's not coming to help you."

Wolff spat again.

"Do. You. See?"

Anna's face fell, and she stared at the floor, but Sig reached out across the space between them and found her hand.

Wolff cleared his throat.

"So, I have a decision to make, and the decision is this: which one of you do I have to shoot to get the other one to tell me where it is?"

30

Sun Day, night

Always tell the truth.
Never lie, for Satan uses lies against us.
Turn the other cheek.
Be good and peaceful and avoid the path to evil.
Forgive your enemies and pray for them.

These were the things Maria had taught her children, and though Sig had been too small to learn much then, it was the same message Nadya had taught them too.

But Nadya had left them, and no one from town had come to help Anna and Sig. There was no one to turn to.

They sat in their chairs, watching Wolff as he made up his mind, occasionally lifting the tip of the Colt first toward one of them, then the other.

Sig's mind was a fury, trying to see a way out of it all, searching for any tiny chink in Wolff's armor, for some clue as to what to say to make it all stop. So many things he had learned. His mother had always taught him to

156

speak the truth and to believe in it as the only path to God, and yet Einar had kept the truth from them for years and landed them in this mess. Only now did they understand why Einar had chosen to live six miles from town, to isolate themselves from other human contact.

"Know everything you can know," his father used to say, but sickeningly Sig wondered if he had ever really known his father, and if he didn't know him, how could he love him?

Anna was exhausted, her single thought of her father. Seeing his shape under the blanket rekindled all sorts of awful memories. She was just ten again, seeing her mother lying in a pool of her own blood.

Her doll.

She'd never had another toy since. As she thought about her mother, she remembered the story of Job again, and it brought tears to her eyes as she wondered how her mother could believe in it. How Job had seen his whole life destroyed, and yet had still had faith in the goodness of God.

"Enough!" Wolff said abruptly. He pulled back the hammer on the Colt with his one thumb.

Time slowed to a crawl as Sig had a brief premonition of the future, the very near future. When Wolff moved his forefinger less than a quarter of an inch, that hammer would fall and ignite the primer in the cartridge. The powder would burn, burn so fast as to be an explosion, but all contained inside the tiny brass case of the cartridge, just as Einar had explained all those years ago. He heard his father's voice once more, as if he were there. Telling him how the metal would expand, to press against the walls of the cylinder, releasing the lead of the bullet, which would begin its spinning journey toward him. Or Anna. Either was equally awful to think about.

Before the bullet struck, that little brass case would have cooled enough and shrunk enough so that next time Wolff loaded the gun, it would slip lightly out of the cylinder.

Wolff spoke slowly.

"I choose you."

He pointed the gun at Sig.

"Wait!" Sig screamed. "Wait. I've thought of something."

There was just enough conviction in his voice for Wolff to hear him out.

31

Sun Day, night

"**B**e very careful you don't play games with me, boy."
Sig spoke desperately, genuinely, hurriedly.

"I'm not. We don't know about this gold, I promise we
don't, but if you say father had it then it must be
somewhere. And we don't have it here. We'd know. It's a
tiny place. Supposing Father had put it in the bank? In
cash. He had an account at the mining bank. If he had,
there'd be papers. We could get them and give the money
to you. Just let us go. We'll give you the money."

"Sig's right," Anna said. "There were papers on the
sled when we found him. You said yourself he'd cleaned
everything out of his office. He must have been bringing
them home. There might be something in those
papers."

"Nonsense," Wolff growled, and lowered his gaze at Sig
again.

"No!" cried Anna. "It's true. They're on the ice. His

159

papers. Don't you want to go and look at least? Then we can give you the gold and you can leave."

Wolff's gun hovered like a cobra waiting to strike. The tip of the barrel made circles in the air as Wolff tried to think straight.

"Maybe," he said eventually. "Maybe you're right. Where are these papers now? On the ice where you found him?"

"We left them. We didn't think they mattered. We just wanted to get Father back to the hut. We threw everything else off the sledge and got the dogs to get us back as fast as we could."

"You left them?"

"I swear we did," Sig cried. "I swear on my life."

"So they're out there?"

"In the snow, on the ice. There's a leather bag, and a lot of papers. We could go and get them."

Wolff went to the window. He stared into the dark.

"Yes," he said. "We could go and get them. But not now. At first light. And if you're lying to me, boy . . ."

"I swear it. I swear I'm not lying. On my life."

"Not on your life," Wolff said, and now he wasn't smiling anymore. He looked at Anna where she sat, and once again his eyes devoured the beauty in front of him.

"On hers."

32

Moon Day, dawn

With the passing of the night, there came time. A long, aching, hurting time, cursed and forlorn, in which there was nothing to do but think.

They spent the night sitting on the unforgiving wooden chairs, till their muscles ached and their backs were in agony, yet Wolff had stayed almost motionless on his chair, across the cabin from them. His eyes were slits in the half light from the oil lamp, almost shut, and Sig and Anna had no idea if he could see them, or whether he was asleep. Then, desperate to stretch his aching legs, Sig tried to stand and found the revolver pointing straight at him again.

He sat down hurriedly.

Sig's mind drifted back, from the day trapped in the cabin with Wolff, to finding Einar on the ice and then farther still, until, unbidden, he found himself looking at the whole of his short life and wondering what any of it

161

meant. All he felt was that same feeling he'd always had, that he was looking for something, whose name he didn't even know, and yet now, in the dark of the night, and with his father gone to wherever his mother had gone before, with Anna sitting beside him, he suddenly knew its name.

Home.

They tried to whisper to each other a couple of times, trying to say things that it couldn't hurt for Wolff to hear.

Sig wanted to know about Nadya.

"Has she really gone? Why?"

"I'm so sorry, Sig," Anna whispered back. "I'm sorry. Listen, Sig. Remember. I'll never leave you."

But there was an awful implication in what she said, in the presence of the gun that lay on Wolff's lap across the room.

They fell silent, and though it came hard, at some point Sig knew he must have slept, even sitting in that chair, for he woke to see Wolff judging the light from the window.

"It's time to go," he said.

Anna and Sig looked at each other and stiffly got to their feet, their legs and backs aching.

"Not you," Wolff said, looking at Anna.

"What do you mean?" she said.

"I'm not going to take both of you out on the ice. I

162

don't like those odds. You're going to stay here while I take the boy. And I'm sure you can be trusted to stay here. Can't you?"

Anna nodded dumbly.

"Lying bitch," Wolff snarled. "How stupid do you think I am? Boy, you got some rope in that storeroom of yours?"

Sig knew they had. Lots of it. It hung on a hook underneath the shelf where the coffee tins were kept. And behind the coffee tins . . .

He nodded.

"Yes, I think so."

"Then go and get it."

He waved the gun at the door to the room, to the storeroom beyond it, and Sig hurried. His heart began to race before he'd even left the room; he could almost hear Einar's gun calling to him now. Though he couldn't see clearly what he should do, with a brief but sudden shock, Sig knew that somewhere during the night he had stopped deciding whether to use the gun or not. He had made up his mind, and there was only one question that remained; whether he'd get the single chance he needed.

Before he knew it he was in the hall, opening the door into the storeroom.

He knew he didn't have long. Wolff would expect him straight back, or he'd know something was wrong.

Sig stood in the near dark, and his heart thumped even harder in his chest, as he wondered if he could actually take the gun out of its box, walk next door, and shoot Wolff.

It sounded so easy, but his pounding heart told him it was not. Wolff had his gun in his hand, a gun he had fired many hundreds of times, no doubt. Sig had only ever fired a gun once, that time on his birthday. Even with the slight surprise, the chances were that Sig would wind up dead and then Anna, too.

He was wasting time.

He pushed the coffee tins aside and grabbed the Colt's box. He turned to the door and set it on the lid of a barrel of dried beans that stood there, trying to get a bit more light.

Then he had an idea. He reached up to the hook and took down a large coil of rope. He'd carry it in front of him, and it would conceal the gun for a crucial second, and then, he just had to pull the trigger. Just once.

He turned back to the door and saw Wolff framed in the doorway.

"What's keeping you?"

"N-nothing," stammered Sig, desperately trying not to look at the Colt box. It was inches from Wolff, and yet in the gloom, he hadn't seen it. Wolff kept glancing back into the cabin to keep an eye on Anna, too.

"Got the rope?"

He peered back into the darkness. Sig stumbled out of the storeroom.

"It's dark in there," he muttered, trying to excuse the time he'd taken. A few seconds too many, that was all.

And if he *had* hidden the gun under the coil of rope, what then? Sig pushed the thought away. The chance had gone.

Back in the cabin, Wolff sent Sig to stand by the far wall, while he motioned with the revolver for Anna to sit down again.

Keeping one eye on Sig, Wolff placed the gun on the floor beside Anna's chair, out of the reach of her foot. He took the coil of rope and began to wind it tight around her wrists, tying them to the back of the chair, then continuing to loop the rope around her waist and the back of the chair.

He leaned right into her as he did and pulled violently on the rope, so that she gasped a couple of times. That seemed to make Wolff pull even harder, and he lingered, enjoying the act of binding her. His hands pawed her body, and his fingers stroked her dress here and there as they went, pushing into the soft flesh underneath.

Anna shut her eyes, and Sig swore silently under his breath.

Then it was over.

Her whole body was bound fast, her back to the chair back, her legs to the chair's legs.

Wolff dragged the chair into the middle of the room, well away from any possible object or aid, so that she faced the window.

165

Then he seemed to change his mind, and he rotated it ninety degrees, so that Anna sat looking at the body of her father on the table.

"To remind you not to do anything foolish," Wolff said.

He looked at Sig.

"Put your gloves on, boy," he snapped. "We're going out on the ice."

At the door, Sig turned and looked despairingly at his sister.

But she was not looking at him. Instead, as Wolff pushed Sig through the door, she called to him.

"You killed my mother, didn't you?"

Wolff stiffened.

"I never had the pleasure of knowing your mother," he said, and then they were gone.

33

Moon Day, early morning

You cannot see the future. You cannot hear what has not yet been said, nor do the days that have yet to be have any place in the huddled collection of memories which fight for your attention.

And yet as Sig left the cabin that morning with Wolff and set off across the frozen lake, he could feel the presence of things that were about to become reality, and it scared him so much that he became short of breath.

It was a bright morning but cold enough to chill a man's soul, and nothing stirred. Nothing. They tramped down from the porch, sending a large icicle crashing onto the boards beside them. Fighting against the relentless assault from the cold, they pulled their coats tight as they went, Sig in front, Wolff behind. He still held the gun, now under a blanket he'd thrown over his shoulders to swathe his upper body. His greatcoat swung out beneath like the skirt of a dress, and all in all Wolff looked like a deadly scarecrow.

"Far?" he barked at Sig.

Sig looked across the ice. There was no snow falling, and he fancied he could even see the spot from here, a small brown smudge on the ice a way out, though it was hard to be sure.

"Half a mile. Maybe a mile."

"We'll take your dogs," Wolff said, and Sig nodded.

It seemed a lifetime since he and Anna and Nadya had hurtled back up the slope from the lake with Einar's body on the sled, and then his sister and stepmother had taken the dogs back into Giron.

They were pleased to see Sig now but looked tired, and when they saw he had still not brought them any food, they began to howl and whine.

"Shut them up," Wolff barked. "Or I shoot them."

Sig comforted the four dogs as best he could and began to harness them. They were working dogs and the feel of the harness pleased them, enough to take their minds off food for a while longer. It was a job that should have been easy, and in warmer weather would have been so, but in the extreme cold it became a long and torturous job as he fumbled with stiff leather straps and brass buckles with his clumsy gloved hands.

"Hurry," grunted Wolff angrily from behind him. Sig didn't even have to look to know that the revolver was pointing at the back of his neck. Somehow he could feel it.

"Quiet there. Shh now," he cooed to Fram, the lead, and as she fell silent, so did her team.

Sig fixed the harness to the sled and took Fram by her collar to lead the dogs out of the dog hut.

After a short run down to the shore, open ice lay before them.

Sig drove the team, standing on the runners at the back, and Wolff sat backward on the empty bed of the sled, facing Sig. The blanket covered him like a shroud, but there was an angle, a lump in the blanket, and Sig knew it was the gun.

It reminded him of something his father had once told him about guns and very cold weather, but he couldn't exactly remember the details. It was something to do with taking a gun from a very, very cold place into the warm, but maybe it was the other way around. He wished he could remember, but he did recall his father saying that if you did this, the metal of the gun would "sweat," as condensation formed on its surface, and that then the gun could rust or seize up or even misfire. But he had no idea whether this happened in seconds or minutes or days.

If Wolff had no gun . . . well, that would even things up a little. Just a little.

Sig cracked the whip, gently once, in the air above

Fram's nose. She was a good dog and was away immediately, heading straight onto the ice.

If Wolff showed any concern at suffering the same fate as Einar, he didn't show it. He was almost nonchalant as he rode like a backwards-facing Buddha on the frozen water, his head lolling from the jolting of the sled.

Sig's fears were also more pressing than the possibility of the ice breaking, as he kept one eye on his dogs and the other on the gun under the blanket. But as they came closer to the brown smudge he'd seen from the shore, and saw it was indeed Einar's stuff from the sled, he found himself picturing his father's terrible end again.

The cold ate at them both now, despite the years each had spent in the miles north of the Arctic Circle. Sig felt weak from hunger; he had had barely any food. Lack of sleep made him feel sick, and the freezing air grabbed his lungs with every breath, every one a lungful of ice crystals, sucking his body heat away some more.

Wolff stared at Sig, his eyes unblinking.

Sig's hands clung to the ganglines, but in reality he was not guiding the dogs. Fram knew where they were going, to a small disturbed patch in the ice, slightly clearer of snow, and the few things that lay there.

Sig pulled them in slightly, and even as he did, the ice gave a warning, a menacing creaking sound that chilled his heart. His eyes darted about to this side of the sled and that, waiting for a telltale splinter to open up, but none came and the creaking was behind them.

They came to the bundles on the ice, and the dogs stopped without Sig having to make them.

"Here?" Wolff said, craning his neck.

He grunted, then motioned with his gun at Sig, telling him to move away from the sledge. He didn't want to be stranded on the ice and give the boy a head start back to the cabin.

Sig understood and dropped the lines over the back of the sledge, then watched Wolff spin and haul his bulk from his sitting position. He stood and edged his way across the ice.

"Good," he said.

There was the leather satchel, just as Sig had said, lying on the ice with its mouth open. A few papers were spilled in the snow, some stuck to the ice now, others maybe had blown away.

Wolff bent to pick up the bag, then tried to gather some of the loose leaves of paper. But though his gloves were thin enough to allow his fingers to fit the trigger guard of a Colt, they were too thick to grasp rigid sheets of paper from the lake ice.

While he scrabbled with the papers, he seemed to forget Sig, and Sig himself had seen something else.

He was looking at the small pile of matches again; the tiny sticks of wood that could have saved his father's life, but hadn't. Then he saw what he had missed in the panic of finding Einar. A book. A black, leather-bound book, lying in the snow, near the tumble of matches.

It was their Bible, the Bible that had been his mother's, and Sig saw it was that which Einar had tried to burn to save his life.

The Bible. Why the Bible? It lay on its open front, the edge of a few pages twitching in the slight breeze from the head of the lake, and Sig understood what his father had been trying to do. Those thin pages, thin, thin like wafers, would have been the easiest to catch alight, and with those burning, Einar might just have had the chance of staying alive.

But the Bible had survived, and Einar had not.

On an impulse Sig bent over and using both hands, scooped the book from the ice, closing its cover.

Immediately Wolff's eyes were on him.

"What's that, boy?"

Sig held it up for him to see.

"Bible," he said, and suddenly from nowhere, Sig found he had more strength than he thought. Maybe it was just the touch of fate brushing his heart, but he found he didn't care if Wolff put a bullet in him there and then.

"My mother's Bible," he added. "I want it."

Wolff glared at him, perplexed, then turned away, and Sig stowed the Bible into the gaping outer pocket of his coat as greedily as if it had been the gold Wolff was searching for.

Suddenly there was a loud groan under their feet, as the ice began to complain about their presence. It subsided quickly, but then another crack came from a few feet away.

"Time to go," Wolff said, and Sig nodded.

They hurried from the scene, Wolff clutching his paper treasure, and Sig his.

The Bible felt like the last link to his parents. It had been his mother's pride, that beautiful black leather-bound book. On the front, the words "HOLY BIBLE" were stamped in gold leaf, and the edges of the pages were also rimmed with gold. He remembered how the book shone in the candlelight when Maria read from it.

More than anything else, it meant his mother. And though she and Einar had argued over what lay inside its pages, just as Einar and Nadya would later, Einar had come to treasure it after her death, keeping it more preciously than anything that was theirs, save perhaps the Colt.

One summer day a year or so ago, Sig had come in from swimming in the lake to find his father working at the cabin table with the Bible, some fresh paper, and a pot of hot glue.

"This old thing's coming to pieces," Einar had said. "Needs some care and attention."

173

Nadya and Anna had come in then too, and Nadya had smiled to see what Einar was doing. She stood behind him while he finished repairing the endpapers, strengthening the cover, then planted a kiss on the top of his head.

"You're a good man, Einar," she said.

Einar had laughed, and waved the finished Bible at Sig.

"As good as the men in here, eh son? Maybe!"

Sig smiled.

"Maybe," he said.

Something seemed to occur to Einar then.

"Even the dead tell stories," he said. "Don't I always say that? Yes? And this book is full of them. Full of them both. Dead men and stories, dead men and stories. You just have to know how to listen."

It seemed to amuse him, and for the rest of that day, there had been nothing but harmony in the Andersson house.

34

Moon Day, morning

God must have smiled on the man and the boy that morning, on the sinner and the innocent, as they made their way back across the ice. Or maybe God wasn't watching. Either way, the ice held, despite frequent warning cracks, sounding like distant gunfire.

Sig ran the dogs as hard as he dared, hoping they would tread lightly on the ice, that their speed would be enough to see them across even a genuine crack. Wolff seemed lost in a world of his own, rummaging through the leather bag, rifling through the papers inside, though on the jolting sled and with gloved hands, Sig doubted he could have read much, if anything, of what lay within.

And if they got back to the cabin, and the papers were all worthless, no bank drafts, or statements of account. What then?

What would Wolff do then?

*

175

Yet things were not to turn out that way, because there was a surprise for Wolff and Sig when they got back to the cabin.

Wolff pushed Sig up the slope in front of him, anxious to be back in the warm, curious to see what secrets Einar's papers held. For the first time, doubt had crept into his mind. Supposing Einar's children were telling the truth? Supposing the old goat had spent it all, or lost it over the years? Supposing the papers held nothing but empty words and symbols? Well, he would take something with him, he knew that much. He wouldn't leave empty-handed.

Sig opened the cabin door, took two steps inside, and stopped dead. Hope leapt into his heart, as Wolff came in behind him and saw the empty chair and the loose bundle of ropes scattered around its feet.

Anna was nowhere to be seen.

"Damn girl," Wolff said, and whirled around, dropping his bundle, expecting to be attacked at any second.

When it didn't come, he swore again and swung a fist at Sig, catching the side of his head. The blow sent Sig reeling, and he was immediately sick on the floor. As he rolled away from the mess, Wolff straddled him, one foot either side of his body. His arm pointed at Sig's head, and at the end of his arm was the revolver. Sig felt something under his hand. The Bible had fallen out of his pocket as he'd dropped to the floor.

"Where is she?" Wolff hissed.

Sig tried to scrabble backward on the floor, but Wolff put a hefty boot on his chest.

"Where is she?"

He pulled the hammer of the gun back.

"I don't know, I don't know, I don't know." The words spilled out of Sig.

Wolff blinked slowly once, and Sig closed his eyes.

There was a crash from behind them. Something had fallen off a shelf in the store room, and in two paces Wolff crossed the room and ducked into the dark.

Sig scrambled to his feet, but before he was even halfway upright, Wolff was back, with Anna clutched by the neck in one big gloved paw. Sig's heart sank. Why hadn't she got away? But instantly he realized what she'd been doing in the store, and he felt sick again.

Wolff hurled Anna across the room, away from him. Biting off his gloves with his teeth, he flung them to the floor, and now they saw him really angry.

He advanced, waving the gun at them, stamping on the floorboards with his heavy boots.

"No more games!" he screamed. "Where is my gold?"

But neither of them answered, because they knew there was no gold for him to have.

"Tell me!" Wolff yelled, and then, "Or I kill you both!"

Still crouching on the floor, Anna put her arm around Sig.

"I'm sorry," she said. "I couldn't find it."

Sig knew what she meant, what she'd been looking for, and hadn't found. She hadn't found it because Sig had moved it to sit on the barrel of beans by the door.

"What?" Wolff snapped. "What's that? You couldn't find what? Is the gold in there? Is that it?"

Anna hung her head.

"No. Not gold."

"Then what? Tell me or I shoot you."

A seed of a thought planted itself in Sig's mind. No. It was more than a seed. It was the birth of something greater, something born from a lifetime of watching and waiting, and without knowing quite why, Sig knew this was his moment. Maybe it was desperation, maybe something more, but there was definitely something wrong with what was going on.

We're dead anyway, he thought. We're dead anyway.

"Why don't you?" he said.

Wolff turned from Anna to Sig.

"What?" he said, snarling.

"Why don't you shoot?" Sig said. "You keep threatening to. Why don't you?"

He got to his feet.

"Sit down!" Wolff thrust the gun at Sig, but Sig stayed standing.

"Shoot me," he said, as calm as the depths of the forest. For a brief, strange but wonderful moment he was filled with elation.

Wolff hesitated for a second, then smashed the revolver into the side of Sig's head.

He went down, his eyes saw nothing more.

35

Moon Day, morning

Does God turn his eyes away when bad things happen? Or does he watch, wondering at how his creation unfolds? Does he shake his head in sorrow? Or does he smile?

Sig lay on the floor of the cabin, not moving.

Anna screamed.

"You've killed him! You . . . You've killed him!"

She wailed and tried to scramble across the floor to Sig, but Wolff moved into her path, squatting down in front of her.

"I hope so," he drawled.

She slapped him viciously across the face, so that her hand stung, and yet Wolff seemed almost not to notice.

"Now then," he said, and Anna saw the darkness come into his eyes. She began to stumble away, staggering to her feet as she went, but Wolff was on her.

"Please . . ." Anna began.

"What?" mocked Wolff. "Please don't kill me? After ten years, ten years of waiting. Of hunting and travelling and freezing and almost damn-well dying, and you don't have my gold? Please don't kill me? Oh, I'm not going to kill you. Not yet. I want something for my trouble."

Anna felt the back of her calves press against the edge of the bed, and Wolff towered in front of her.

"Not yet," he whispered, as he pushed her backward.

Anna began to cry, as terrible memories flooded back.

"You killed my mother!" she screamed. "You killed my mother!"

Wolff paused, gazing at the girl on the bed in front of him.

"Come now," he said, licking his lips. "Let's not speak of the snow that fell last year."

36

Moon Day, morning

Not feeling anything, not hearing anything, Sig nonetheless opened his eyes and what he saw made him want to howl.

Not just Anna lying on the bed, with Wolff standing over her, tugging at his waistband. Not just the shape of his father's corpse under the blanket, not the pool of his own blood in which he lay, flowing freely from the wound to his head.

Even the dead tell stories. Stories of lies, and lies of stories, and lying, lying in blood, Sig leaked his life out, glaring at the man who told him that the dead can speak. His own dead now, his father, lying no more, but lying frozen on the table.

It made him want to howl.

But he didn't.

As he saw Wolff stroke one hand up the length of Anna's leg, he turned away and bolted for the door.

From the corner of his eye, he saw Wolff spin around, but nothing would stop Sig now. He flung himself around the frame of the door and into the storeroom.

The gun box was gone, but immediately he saw it on the floor—that had been the sound that had given Anna away, as she'd clumsily knocked it to the floor, the very thing she'd been looking for. Its contents were strewn across the floorboards.

He grabbed the revolver, and heard steps coming across the cabin.

But the gun was not kept loaded. He needed cartridges, and they had spilled. He fumbled for them frantically, and sent them clattering away from him.

He tried again, but there was only time to snatch one of the little brass tubes from the floor.

He flicked the chamber gate open with shaking hands, slid the cartridge in, snapped the cylinder around into place, and stood.

The door darkened.

"Get back!" Sig screamed, and Wolff froze where he was.

"Get back!" Sig yelled again, and this time Wolff edged back into the cabin, his own gun leveled at Sig's chest.

"What are you doing?" Wolff said evenly, but Sig ignored him, kept edging him back into the room.

"Keep going," he said. "Anna, are you all right?"

Anna got up from the bed, smoothing her skirts, her

eyes meeting Sig's then opening wide as she saw the gun in his hands.

"What are you doing with that, boy?" Wolff asked again. "That old piece of your Pappa's? You going to hurt somebody with that?"

"Be quiet, Wolff," Sig said, pointing the gun straight toward him. "Anna, come away from him."

"Now wait a minute," Wolff said. "Wait a minute."

"What's wrong with your gun, Wolff?" Sig said, his breath coming in nervous gasps. Once more he watched himself as if from outside, heard himself speak as if it were someone else speaking, and as he did, he felt his strength growing and his voice becoming calmer. "What's wrong with your gun? You've been waving it around an awful lot. But I don't think you're going to use it, are you? I think there's something wrong with it. Isn't that right? Because otherwise I think we'd both be dead by now."

Sig saw in the silence which followed that he was right. A fury swept into Wolff's eyes as he realized he'd been found out, and it seemed he would paw the floor like a bull in barely contained rage.

"What happened to it? Did the cold get to it? Did you let it get too cold? Did it rust when you stayed at some inn someplace? You should leave a gun outside when it's been in the cold. You should know that."

He stared straight into Wolff's eyes, and though Wolff held his gaze, Sig no longer felt afraid.

184

Wolff smiled.

"Smart boy," he said. "Just like your damn father. Too damn smart."

Wolff lowered his hand, and when it was pointing at the floor, he let his useless barrel-rusted gun drop to the floor, where it lay like a dying beast, no hint of danger left about it.

"Anna," Sig said. "Are you all right? Did he touch you?"

Anna moved over to Sig.

"I'm okay," she said. "All right." But she wouldn't look at Wolff.

"How did you get free?" Sig asked. "Nadya's here, isn't she?"

Anna nodded.

"I couldn't tell you. Not in front of him. She left just before you got back. She's gone for help. Proper help, this time."

"Good," Sig said. "Now, I want you to go after her, catch her up. Take the dogs and catch her up."

"Sig . . ."

"Please, Anna, do as I say."

Sig didn't take his eyes off Wolff, but he spoke urgently and insistently to Anna.

"Please. For my sake. For your sake. For Pappa," he paused. "For Mother. Do as I ask. Please?"

Anna waited a long time before answering and even then her answer was only a nod.

185

She went to the door, pulling gloves and a coat on.

"Sig," she said.

"Yes?"

"Remember your mother. Remember her, remember what she would tell you now."

"Listen to your sister, boy," Wolff whispered. "She's right. Once you pull that trigger, your life will never be the same again. It won't just be my life you're ending, boy."

But Sig didn't answer, didn't answer either of them, and Anna shut the door behind her.

She was halfway across the snow towards the dog huts, when she heard the shot.

A single shot, which rang out across the whole of the frozen valley, from the cabin to Giron.

The echo of the shot came back, shaking the snow from the tops of the trees, and the ravens took wing.

37

Moon Day, morning

Love.

Faith, Hope, and Love. That was what Maria had tried to teach her children, but she had died too soon to finish their education.

In some move of the hand of fate, or maybe of God, Nadya had entered their lives to finish that teaching, but still, these are lessons for which you have to provide your own answers. That much, Sig had learned.

In the cabin, Sig stood staring at the tip of the barrel of his father's old Colt. The smoke from the black powder cartridge curled into the air. He breathed deeply. To pull the trigger, or not to pull the trigger? It was such a tiny act, such a small difference between doing it and not doing it. So small a choice, was there really any difference at all? And yet there was, and he had chosen to pull the trigger. It was easy.

187

Wolff sat on the floor, against the wall, the wall that now bore a blasted hole almost a foot wide in its surface, about two feet away from Wolff's head.

"Why?" Wolff asked. "You could have won."

He stood up.

"You could have won. Why did you miss?"

Sig smiled.

"My mother's children are not murderers," he said, and handed the empty gun to Wolff. Without another word, he turned and walked toward the cabin door.

Wolff stared at him open-mouthed, and then at the gun in his hands.

His left hand moved to the string of shiny new cartridges clipped into a belt around his waist, and with almost childlike glee he eased one out of the leather and slid it into Einar's old gun.

Sig heard him do it.

He had reached the door and opened it.

He didn't falter as he heard Wolff thumb the hammer back on the revolver. It clicked into place and Sig knew that it was held back from falling onto the primer only by a tiny sliver of metal.

He prayed, but he didn't pray to God.

He prayed to his mother; he prayed that she wasn't wrong to preach the path of peace.

He prayed to his father; he prayed that his father had known what he was talking about when he said that you should never put a powerful new smokeless cartridge into an old gun like theirs.

He heard the trigger grate. There was a second deafening bang as the gun roared into life again, some of the roof splintered down onto Sig, and with it came a scream of wild pain. The gun had blown apart, taking half of Wolff's hand off with it.

38

Moon Day, morning

Anyone would have thought it was the Devil himself who came flying out of the cabin after Sig, as he bolted down from the porch.

He saw Anna ahead, transfixed by the two gun shots.

"Run!" he shouted.

She didn't need telling twice.

Behind Sig, Wolff staggered like a drunk, as rage and pain fought for control of his mind and his body. Blood was pouring from his right hand; the thumb and at least his first two fingers were gone, and he clutched uselessly at it with his thumbless left.

"Run!"

Sig waved Anna on, but soon caught her up.

He risked a look backward, and to his horror he saw Wolff was gaining on them.

He seemed oblivious to his injury, just wanting one thing now. He had forgotten about gold, about revenge, about lust. All he wanted to do was kill them both, and Sig did not doubt that even in his wounded state, he could still do that.

Anna turned for the shore, but Sig called her back.

"No! This way. Up here. To the trees."

They put on a burst of speed that took them to the line of little trees that lay at the edge of the forest, and then Anna saw what Sig saw.

The snow.

"Wait!" Sig cried. "Anna. Wait. We need to walk."

"What?" Anna cried. "Are you mad?"

"No! Anna, remember! We need to walk!"

And now Anna nodded and stopped.

Wolff was only yards away.

"Have faith," she said to herself, and walked across the snow.

Sig followed, trying to stop himself from breaking into a run.

Slowly, they set out across the snow field between the trees.

They were maybe twenty feet in when Wolff hurtled after them. It was enough. Within two paces he sank into the snow up to his chest, breaking through the ice crust which Sig and Anna had walked clean over.

He floundered, waving his arms around him, blood staining the snow in a vivid red scar all around him.

At one moment it seemed he might break free, but his

rage and his strength were draining away with his blood.

Sig and Anna walked on a few more paces, then stopped and turned.

It was true.

Wolff was trapped.

"Help me!" he cried. "Help me. I'm hurt."

Sig remembered. He remembered saying the same thing to Wolff, only hours before. What was it Wolff had said in reply?

Sig took a tentative step closer to him.

"Well, Mr. Wolff," he whispered. "Is that my problem?"

1967

The Warwick Hotel
New York City

Postscript

Sigfried Andersson sat in the small but elegant bar of the hotel and recalled the last of the story. He was chatting to a young soldier who had just come back from a war in a jungle in a country Sig had never heard of. The young soldier had seen some sights, and had heard some stories, but he'd never heard a story like the one the old Swedish man was telling him.

Some of the details were crystal clear, some were hazy; it had been a long time. He'd forgotten some of it, but then, there were times when he forgot for a moment the name of the woman he'd married, though she'd only been dead five years.

He was an old man, and old men have a right to forget certain things.

But there were other things he would never forget.

He would never forget dragging Wolff from the snow, with Anna's help, and then Nadya's, too. Mr. Bergman and men from town arrived soon afterward, and took Wolff away. He wasn't quite dead, and even to this day Sig couldn't work out exactly how he felt about that. He'd heard that Wolff had died in prison a few years later, in a fight with another prisoner. The dumb man had never learned to control his anger, and it had cost him his life in the end. A man with no thumbs was never going to win a fight with a cell mate holding an iron table leg.

And then there was something else that he would never forget. Anna and Nadya and he had gone back into the cabin, to try and set things right. The men from town had taken Einar's body away, in preparation for the funeral, and the three Anderssons had gone with them, staying at Per Bergman's house till it was done.

There was time for grief then, at last, and some kind words were spoken that settled the anger between Anna and Nadya for good. Then the time came to return to the cabin, and Sig, for one, went with great dread. The cabin looked just the same as ever from outside, but inside the signs of the struggle were still evident.

They'd cleaned up the mess, lit the stove, put on some food to cook. Anna had set the chairs on their feet, and Sig saw their mother's Bible lying on the floor.

As he picked it up, his father's words came into his head.

"Even the dead tell stories," Einar had said, "and this book is full of them."

Finally something clicked in Sig's head. He pictured the day Einar had repaired Maria's Bible. Opening the front cover, he saw what no one had seen before. A slight bulge, flat and square, under the endpaper. He understood that Einar had not meant to burn the Bible at all but, knowing he was already dead, had tried to draw their attention to it.

He took the knife from Nadya's hand as she chopped a potato, and she and Anna crowded wordlessly around Sig as he slit open the binding at the front of the Bible.

Two neatly folded squares of paper fell out from inside. One was a short note.

I have something for all of you, but I have hidden it until I know it is safe for you to have it. One day, a man will come. And only when he has gone again, will it be safe for you to have it. When he has gone, take this map and start a new life. I know you can do this, for you are all wonderful and clever people. My Nadya, my Anna, my Sig.

I love you all, E.

The other square of paper was a hand-drawn map. It led them through a path into the forest behind the cabin, to the bole of a huge birch tree, under whose spreading roots they found a steel box.

Inside the box was a small fortune in gold.

It had been years until they'd found out how he'd done it; how he'd smuggled all that gold from right under everyone's noses, grain by grain all through that season. One day Sig had bumped into an old miner from the Alaskan gold rush, who'd told him about all the dodges under the sun, including the one about how gold dust will stick to damp fingers, which can then be transferred unseen to hair that's been slicked carefully through with hair oil, to be washed out every evening into a bowl, strained with a muslin cloth. Just the thought of it had brought the smell of his father's hair back to him, so many years later.

It hadn't been so very much money really, but they'd spent it wisely, after convincing Nadya that there was not really anything else they could do with it. They'd bought a stake in Per Bergman's mine, and in the end the iron business had made them very rich.

Just then, Anna came down the stairs and into the hotel bar. She smiled when she saw her brother, still so very much her little brother, even though he was seventy-two.

She laughed as she joined Sig and the young soldier.

"Still telling that old story," she said.

Sig nodded.

"Time to go," Anna said. "The concert won't wait for us, and I don't want to miss it."

They bade the soldier good-bye.

As they walked arm in arm to the concert hall a couple of streets away, Anna turned to Sig.

"You know," she said. "It took me years to work out why you did it."

"What's that?" Sig said, though he could guess.

"Why you let Wolff have the gun. When you knew he had more bullets."

"Ah, that," said Sig. "Well, it was what you said to me, as you left the cabin. I suddenly saw what I had to do. I wanted to be true to our mother, but I didn't want to let our father down either. And I saw a way to do both, to make them both happy."

"But you risked your life to do it."

"Maybe," said Sig.

"Or were you trusting in God's intervention?"

Sig stopped for a moment. He shrugged.

"I was trusting in what our parents taught us, in their own different ways. Luckily for me, it worked."

Anna smiled.

"You know, I understand it now. There's always a third choice in life. Even if you think you're stuck between two impossible choices, there's always a third way. You just have to look for it."

199

Sig said nothing, but nodded and walked on, and Anna with him.

That night, as Sig went to sleep with the music of Mahler still drifting around his head, two thoughts came to him.

The first thought was this: that he was a foolish old man, because all his life he'd been looking for something, and it was only when Anna joined him in the bar that evening that he realized that home is not something you find outside yourself; home is something you carry inside you, and it's made from the memories of the people you love, and the people who have loved you.

As this thought left his head, it took with it a small burden that he'd carried for almost sixty years; as he connected to the child he'd been before Wolff stalked into his life, and in the space of little more than thirty-six hours, had stopped being a boy and started being a man. Was it Wolff who'd killed that boy? Or had Sig just been waiting for the right moment to start the rest of his life? It didn't matter anymore.

The second thing he thought of was something the young soldier had said to him. He'd said that a story like theirs was too good to be forgotten, and that what Sig ought to do was to write it down. Sig had replied that he couldn't do it. Or rather, not that he couldn't, but that it wouldn't feel right, writing about himself.

So the young soldier, who was himself hoping to be a writer, explained that Sig could write the story as if he was writing it about someone else, about some other family.

Sig understood.

So one day, I picked up a pen, and a small black notebook, and that's just what I did.

And now it's finished, I hope you liked my story.

Sigfried Andersson
New York City

Author's Note

When I decided to make a revolver and the Arctic Circle the central themes of my novel I thought I had better know what I was writing about, and once again I must thank my wonderful publisher for her belief in and support for the book I hoped to write.

It was in sub-zero temperatures in Northern Sweden that I got a sense of the cold and the landscape and walked on frozen lakes. It was there, in Swedish Lapland, that I came across the story of a revivalist preacher, the model for Nadya's preacher, and though this thread in the book has been greatly reduced in the writing, I'd like to thank Lina Moet for her history of the Swedish-Finnish border at the turn of the last century.

For a technical discussion on the revolver, I am greatly indebted to Peter Smithurst of the Royal Armouries, the UK's leading expert on Colts. He carefully explained the history and workings of the Colt, took a 44-40 to pieces for me to show how it works, and did it all with great enthusiasm.

Thanks too to Gunilla Carlsson for checking my Swedish. I will, in turn, try harder to be a better student!

Finally, I decided I should know what it's actually like to fire a live weapon. Since this is not something easily done in the UK, I traveled to Estonia, where retired policeman Tonu Adrik showed me the ropes one January day in sub-zero conditions.

If I had expected firing a gun to be frightening or difficult, I was wrong. The only scary thing about firing a gun is just how easy it is. Too, too easy. I was also struck by the strong desire I had to do it again, which is also a chilling thing to realize.

I think it's up to each of us to decide whether guns are good or bad, just as it is for Sig in the book. Many people argue that a gun does nothing without someone deciding to pull the trigger, but the arguments are too involved to discuss here properly. All I would like to say is that I believe there's always a third option in life, it's just that sometimes it takes a little while to find it.

Marcus Sedgwick
Christmas Day, 2008
Stockholm

GOFISH

QUESTIONS FOR THE AUTHOR

MARCUS SEDGWICK

Kate Christer

What did you want to be when you grew up?
I had no idea. I had vague ideas about being a cat burglar, but that didn't work out. It's just as well I realized about writing in the end, or I might be in jail now.

When did you realize you wanted to be a writer?
I was about twenty-something, I think, though I had always liked writing.

What's your first childhood memory?
Believe it or not, being pushed in a pushchair through the graveyard in the village where I grew up by our nanny . . .

What's your most embarrassing childhood memory?
There are simply too many, and they are too embarrassing to think of let alone write down. . . .

As a young person, who did you look up to most?
My brother

What was your worst subject in school?
Chemistry. I just did not get it, at all.

What was your best subject in school?
Mathematics. No, honestly.

What was your first job?
I taught English in Poland.

How did you celebrate publishing your first book?
I'm not sure I did. . . . Maybe it's time to put that right.

Where do you write your books?
I have a glorified shed in the garden, heated by a wood-burning stove. It's very cozy.

When you finish a book, who reads it first?
My editor. It's her opinion that matters the most.

Are you a morning person or a night owl?
More morning. That's when I write. Afternoons are for naps. Evenings are for fun.

What's your idea of the best meal ever?
That's hard. But any meal with a decent red wine is okay with me.

Which do you like better: cats or dogs?
Dogs. Sadly, I'm away too much to make it practical to have one.

What do you value most in your friends?
Kindness, trustworthiness, humor

SQUARE FISH

Where do you go for peace and quiet?
Home. I live in a tiny village, and it's always wonderful to get back to my little cottage and hide.

What makes you laugh out loud?
My daughter's bad jokes

What's your favorite song?
That's too hard! I could do you a top one hundred. Or maybe a top two hundred . . . I love all sorts of different types of music and always have music playing when I work.

Who is your favorite fictional character?
Mr. Flay from Mervyn Peake's Gormenghast trilogy

What are you most afraid of?
Not wanting to write anymore

What time of year do you like best?
Autumn. No, summer. No wait, spring. No . . . I've got it now! Winter! Which is my way of saying I love all the seasons, and I like that I live in a part of the world where you get to see all four. I love cold countries though, and snow, so if I had to pick one . . .

What's your favorite TV show?
I don't watch TV. I prefer to watch a good film, or even a bad film, over TV.

If you were stranded on a desert island, who would you want for company?
Honestly? I can pick anyone? I'm going to have to think about that for a while.

If you could travel in time, where would you go?
That's really hard! Everywhere maybe. All those amazing periods in history to go to. And that's not even to mention the future . . .

What's the best advice you have ever received about writing?
"Nobody knows anything."

What do you want readers to remember about your books?
The titles would be a good start! And after that, if they remembered what it felt like to read them that would be good too.

What would you do if you ever stopped writing?
Be sad, bereft, beleaguered. And I'd try to make music instead.

What do you like best about yourself?
I don't give up easily.

What is your worst habit?
I say "Okay" too much. And when I say too much, I mean almost all the time.

Where in the world do you feel most at home?
Home. Obviously. And Sweden. Not so obviously.

What do you wish you could do better?
Play the piano. That would be wonderful.

SQUARE FISH

Some secrets are best left unspoken. Rebecca spends the
summer in a seaside town, where she discovers that Ferelith
is ready to tell all and a priest descends into darkness.

Marcus Sedgwick's

White Crow

is both thought-provoking and intensely terrifying.

REBECCA

She could have been anyone.

She could have been any girl who arrived in Winterfold that summer.

That sounds strange, doesn't it?

It sounds strange to my ears, anyway. Summer in Winterfold. How can there ever be any other season here but winter, with a name like that? But whatever the time of year, Winterfold has a cold embrace and, like the snows of winter, it does not let you go easily.

Once upon a time there was a whole town here, not just a handful of houses. A town with twelve churches and thousands of people, dozens of streets, and a busy harbor.

And then the sea ate it.

Storm by storm, year by year, the cliffs collapsed into the advancing sea, taking the town with it, house by house and street by street, until all that was left was a triangle of three streets, a dozen houses, an inn, a church. Well, most of it . . .

And then, that summer, she arrived. And actually I'm lying.

She couldn't have been anyone, because the moment I saw her beautiful face I knew I loved her, and I knew she would love me, too.

I knew.

Rebecca slides out of her father's car and the first thing she notices is the smell.

She sniffs the air and, without knowing it, tries to break it all down. She gets some of it. She gets the hot salty air of the seaside, the tar of the fishing boats hauled up on the beach just out of sight over the ridge, the marram grass of the marshes inland, the hot engine oil because her father has hauled the old car all the way from Greenwich to this God-forgotten place.

She pulls back a long curl of hair blown into her face by the stiff breeze from the shore. Her father pops the trunk of the car and grabs both of her bags at once.

The tiny cottage, idiotically named The Mansion, is disappointing; dark, with low ceilings.

Her father drops the bags on a shabby rug, kicks the door shut behind him with the heel of his boot.

"Well," he says, but Rebecca already doesn't want to hear. She knows what's coming next. "Your home for the next six weeks. Welcome."

He's trying to sound carefree, and opens his arms as if he thinks she'll run into them.

She doesn't. Slowly his arms fall back to his sides.

"Your room's at the top of the stairs. Here, I'll show you."

"I'll find it," Rebecca says, taking her bags. She turns her back on him, though even as she does so she hates herself.

Her room is a little better than downstairs. She drops her stuff and goes to the window, pulling her backpack off as she does and throwing it on the bed.

There is the sea.

Just beyond the ridge that slopes up to the right to become the cliffs, there's the beach, and the sea, and it burns brightly blue this afternoon, a diamond sea sparkling in the hot sun.

She turns to her backpack on the bed, knowing she has lost.

For a moment she wonders what exactly it is that she's lost, and decides it's a few different things, though what she feels most is that she's lost the battle to stop hurting herself.

The bag had been between her feet all the way from Greenwich, and yes, they'd had the radio on loud to hide the fact that neither of them was speaking, but even so, she would have heard it.

So she knows that Adam hasn't called, and she knows there's no point looking but, unable to stop herself, she unzips the front pocket and pulls out her phone.

She stares at the blank screen. Nothing. Nothing. No texts. No missed calls.

For a second she tells herself there's probably been no reception since halfway through the journey, but she has a couple of bars.

She knows that he's not interested. She tells herself to be strong, but that lasts for five short heartbeats, and then she pushes redial.

When he answers, he sounds surprised to hear her.

"Becky?"

She hasn't thought what she's going to say, so it comes out, blunt and raw.

"You said you'd call."

"I did."

"No you didn't. You said you'd call. Three days ago."

"I will," he lies, barely trying to sound as though he means it.

"You won't, because I left today," Rebecca stabs. "So you won't be coming around now. You . . ."

"Becky, listen . . . You don't need to . . . Look, I've got to go."

Then there's laughter at the other end of the phone. Several voices. His mates. A girl's high-pitched laughter rises over the babble.

Rebecca holds the phone away from her head as if it's burning her. Slowly, she moves her thumb over the keys and ends the call. She drops the phone on the bed and stares at it for a long minute, then goes downstairs, fingering the silver crucifix Adam gave her for her birthday. It wasn't a religious thing, more a Goth thing.

Until then, she'd always worn a silver heart pendant. It had been given to her by her dad years ago, when Mum had died. He'd told Rebecca it was so she'd always remember he was there for her, that he loved her, even when they weren't to-gether. But when Adam gave her the crucifix, she'd taken off the heart pendant and hadn't worn it since.

Maybe her dad had noticed. Neither of them had said anything about it. She tried not to feel bad about it; she wasn't Daddy's little girl anymore; it was stupid to cling to that kind of stuff anyway.

Her father comes out of the kitchen.

"Nice room, isn't it?"

She opens the front door.

"I'm going out," she says.

"I'll do something quick. For seven. Don't be too long."

But she's already gone, into the hot late afternoon, and she's so preoccupied that she's unaware of the various eyes that are appraising her.

The new girl.

She blinks in the blazing sun, and looks to her left and right. She turns left, and passes the pub. Briefly she notices the sign. The Angel. It's beautiful, handmade, maybe many years old, but someone has freshly repainted it. A beautiful stylized angel, handsome, with blond curling hair and glowing white robes, a golden halo and a golden sword. He stares into the blue-sky corner of the sign, as if staring up to God. His face is serene, and yet full of yearning, too.

The inn marks the end of the street, and here the road turns back inland, up past the ruins of the priory, so she takes the trail down to the beach. She's taken only a few steps when she sees a footpath leading into the darkness of the woods on the cliff.

The beach is full of happy laughing people, sunshine and sea, and joy. All these things feel dead to her. She considers the path up into the darkness, where she can take her pain away from all the brightness, and hide it.

That's the way she chooses.

1798, 7m., 13d.

There arrived a newcomer to Winterfold today, and God-to-tell, that is a rare enough happening, but further to that, something even more remarkable: he has taken the Hall.

At the inn, they say he is French, and his name is indeed French. He is called Dr. Barrieux, but Martha told me that his voice is not foreign, but that he speaks English as Jesus did.

Bless Martha. At least she cooks passably well.

1798, 7m., 27d.

I learned more of our newcomer today, and yes, Grimes at the Angel Inn said to me that indeed he is newly come from France, from Paris. From Paris! To Winterfold! Think on that. From that most recent hotbed of foment and revolution to our sleepy village, a backwater on any map.

He has taken the Hall, Winterfold Hall, even though it has been empty these long years. For sure, Grimes says, he has been placing a great number of orders for supplies, for vittles and drink, for tools and diverse materials, and also various items of function not known to Grimes.

BRING ME TO LIFE

I might have been normal, but if I was I cannot remember that time.

Once, for my birthday, my mother gave me a book of poetry. They were poems of her own, because she was a poet, and she had written a whole cycle of poems about me. The first ones she had written before I was born, when she was pregnant with me, and the others when I was small.

"This is your gift," she said to me. "Your gift from me. It's better than chocolate, or a toy, because no one else has these poems, and they will last forever."

I was eight years old.

I remember that I nodded solemnly.

"Mother," I said, "you are a genius; you are a poet just like Shakespeare. Like him, you have suns, planets, ants, frightening skeletons. I prefer things that are frightening."

I was eight years old when I said that.

Mother smiled, but even as she did I could see sadder things in her eyes behind her smile.

The weekend drags by for Rebecca as she realizes just how little there is to do in Winterfold. Her father, though he has nothing to do, spends the time finding ways of being busy, of being away, of being absent. He goes for long walks, presumably to try and clear his head.

She hardly sees him.

She lies on her bed for hour after hour, killing three books from cover to cover and as she ends each one drops them broken-spined onto the rough, old floorboards.

They collide briefly during mealtimes, until on Tuesday her father's early return to the house forces her out into the heat.

She explores Winterfold. It takes about twenty minutes. She tells herself off for being a silly city girl, and explores it again properly. This time it takes twenty-five.

There's The Street, where their rented cottage is. It nestles halfway along the row, with its back to the sea, a late medieval cottage with two and a half rooms down and two rooms up. No two houses are alike; there are some older cottages, some more recent ones, probably Victorian. It's like a short lesson in the architecture of English villages. The Street runs parallel to the shore, but the sea is almost entirely hidden behind the houses.

At its northern end are the village shop and a junction. A road leads across the marshes to Crowburgh, while The Street doglegs sharply back inland, with one or two expensive old houses dotted down either side. She can hear a garden party in full swing behind a high brick wall, the raucous music at odds with the Englishness of it all.

She turns and walks back along The Street, past The Mansion.

At the southern end is the pub, from where a small dirt road bumbles down to the beach parking lot, where a notice warns that it can get flooded at times of exceptional tide. The sign brings a smile to her face: a solemn diagram of a car half under-water, a stick-man driver standing on its roof waving for help.

Here again, the road turns back sharply inland, running past the entrance to the ruins of the Priory, once thriving, now just ghosts and stones. Farther on are more big houses behind high walls and hedges, until this road meets the one coming from the other end of The Street, and the triangle that is Winterfold is completed.

Rebecca finds herself at the entrance to the path into the woods again, and again she is drawn in.

She notices another, easier path—straighter—running along the back of the woods, but it looks well used, the sort of path dog walkers take to make sure they have a chat with someone. So she chooses the smaller, steeply twisting path into the thin sliver of woods that stands between her and the sea.

She waits a moment as her eyes adjust to the gloom after the bright sunshine of the village, enjoying the sudden cool of the greenness. She retraces her steps from Saturday, but sees a glimpse of blue through the thick undergrowth, and impulsively she pushes off the trail and through elder bushes and nettles.

She finds herself in a new universe just a few paces wide.

What she has found is a clearing in the woods, once probably well inland, but now eaten in half by the cliffs. Behind her, she's hemmed in by a semicircle of densely packed branches and leaves, a wall. She stands on a patch of neatly cropped grass, right up to the point where the land falls away, and beyond that is the infinity of the sea.

It's like a little room, without a roof, and with natural walls and floor, and the best view of the sea anyone could ever have. There ought to be a bench, but there isn't, and somehow that pleases her. She wonders who keeps the grass short, then notices the rabbit droppings everywhere.

The temptation to jump comes on her suddenly.

There is the cliff in front of her, only steps away, and timidly, like a frightened cat, she creeps toward the drop.

She's very close to the edge before she sees just how high the cliff is. She can see the beach below, and she knows it would be enough to kill her if she fell.

She pictures herself stepping off and it makes her head swim, so she creeps back and gazes out at the sea.

It's a unique place, and though she can hear sounds from the village over the rush of the waves on the beach, it feels a million miles from anywhere or anyone.

It's the need for the comfort of childhood that starts her daydreaming. It's a safe thing to do, something that does not rely on her father, or Adam, or anyone else. Happy memories are invincible, protected and protecting, no one can destroy them.

Words drift into her head, images from books. For some reason she's thinking of *Treasure Island*, but she knows why; she's found the best pirate's lookout point that ever was. *Treasure Island, Robinson Crusoe, Swiss Family Robinson.* Then music. She's thinking about the cliffs and a song about blue-birds, but not even realizing she's got two different songs mixed up, the song in her head is Dorothy's from *The Wizard of Oz.*

She remembers the production at little school, smiling, remembering the blue gingham dress that she wore, and wonders if she can still hit those first two notes, a whole octave apart.

Some-where—

She falters, stops, and tries again, louder this time, and hits it perfectly.

Some-where—

And before she can utter another note, the line is finished by a voice behind her.

Over the rainbow, bluebirds fly . . .

Her heart racing, Rebecca spins around, catching her heel on a rabbit hole.

She falls, and knowing the cliff is at her back, her hands flail wildly, grasping for the ground.

She ends up on her side, winded, her head hanging into thin, clear space.

She looks up into the eyes of the strangest-looking girl she's ever seen.

The strange girl says a strange word.

"Ferelith."

Rebecca faints.